A talent emerges...

Suddenly Cal pushed himself off the bench he'd been leaning against and came to stand in front of me. "What do I have behind my back?" he asked.

My brow creased for a second, then I said, "An apple. Green and red." It was as if I had seen it in his hand.

He smiled, and his expressive, gold-colored eyes crinkled at the edges. He brought his hand from around his back and handed me a hard, greenish red apple, with a leaf still attached to its stem.

Feeling awkward and shy, aware of everyone's eyes on me, I took the apple and bit it, hoping the juice wouldn't run down my chin.

"Good guess," Raven said, sounding irritated. It occurred to me that she was probably jonesing for Cal big time.

"It wasn't a guess," Cal said softly, his eyes on me.

. . .

SWEEP

Book of Shadows (BOOK ONE)

The Coven (BOOK TWO)

Blood Witch (BOOK THREE)

Dark Magick (BOOK FOUR)

Awakening (BOOK FIVE)

Spellbound (BOOK SIX)

The Calling (BOOK SEVEN)

Changeling (BOOK EIGHT)

Strife (BOOK NINE)

Seeker (BOOK TEN)

Origins (BOOK ELEVEN)

Eclipse (BOOK TWELVE)

Reckoning (BOOK THIRTEEN)

Full Circle (BOOK FOURTEEN)

Night's Child (SUPER EDITION)

BOOK OF SHADOWS

Book One

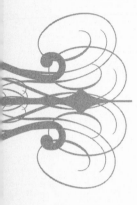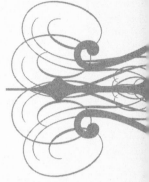

sweep

Cate Tiernan

BOOK OF SHADOWS

speak

An Imprint of Penguin Group (USA) Inc.

All quoted materials in this work were created by the author.
Any resemblance to existing works is accidental.

Book of Shadows

SPEAK
Published by the Penguin Group
Penguin Group (USA) Inc., 345 Hudson Street, New York, New York 10014, U.S.A.
Penguin Group (Canada), 90 Eglinton Avenue East, Suite 700, Toronto, Ontario, Canada M4P 2Y3
(a division of Pearson Penguin Canada Inc.)
Penguin Books Ltd, 80 Strand, London WC2R 0RL, England
Penguin Ireland, 25 St Stephen's Green, Dublin 2, Ireland (a division of Penguin Books Ltd)
Penguin Group (Australia), 250 Camberwell Road, Camberwell, Victoria 3124, Australia
(a division of Pearson Australia Group Pty Ltd)
Penguin Books India Pvt Ltd, 11 Community Centre, Panchsheel Park, New Delhi - 110 017, India
Penguin Group (NZ), 67 Apollo Drive, Mairangi Bay, Auckland 1311, New Zealand
(a division of Pearson New Zealand Ltd)
Penguin Books (South Africa) (Pty) Ltd, 24 Sturdee Avenue, Rosebank, Johannesburg 2196, South Africa

Registered Offices: Penguin Books Ltd, 80 Strand, London WC2R 0RL, England

Published by Puffin Books, a division of Penguin Young Readers Group, 2001
This edition published by Speak, an imprint of Penguin Group (USA) Inc, 2007

9 10 8

Copyright © 2001 17th Street Productions, an Alloy company,
and Gabrielle Charbonnet
All rights reserved

Produced by 17th Street Productions,
an Alloy company
151 West 26th Street
New York, NY 10001

17th Street Productions and associated logos
are trademarks and/or registered trademarks of Alloy, Inc.

Speak ISBN 978-0-14-240986-2

Printed in the United States of America

With love to my life supports
Christine and Marielle

1

Cal Blaire

><"Beware the mage, and bid him well, for he has powers beyond your ken."

—WITCHES, WARLOCKS, AND MAGES,
Altus Polydarmus, 1618><

Years from now I'll look back and remember today as the day I met him. I'll look back and remember the exact moment my life began to include him. I will remember it forever.

I wore a green tie-dyed T-shirt and jeans. My best friend, Bree Warren, arrived in a peasant shirt and a long black skirt down to her violet toenails, and of course she looked beautiful and sophisticated.

"Hey, junior," she greeted me with a hug, even though I'd just seen her the day before.

"See you in AP calc," I told Janice Yutoh, and met Bree halfway down the front steps. "Hey," I said back. "It's hot. It's supposed to be crisp on the first day of school." It wasn't even eight-thirty, but the early September sun was burning whitely, and the air felt muggy and still. Despite the weather I felt excited, expectant: A whole new year was starting, and we were finally upperclassmen.

"Maybe in the Yukon Territory," Bree suggested. "You look great."

"Thanks," I said, appreciating her diplomacy. "You too."

Bree looks like a model. She's tall, five-nine, and has a figure most girls would starve themselves for, except Bree eats everything and thinks dieting is for lemmings. She has minky dark hair that she usually gets styled in Manhattan, so it falls in perfectly tousled waves to the base of her neck. Wherever we go, people turn their heads to look at her.

The thing about Bree is that she knows she's gorgeous, and she enjoys it. She doesn't shrug off compliments, or complain about her looks, or pretend she doesn't know what people are talking about. But she isn't exactly conceited, either. She just accepts what she looks like and thinks it's cool.

Bree glanced over my shoulder at Widow's Vale High. Its redbrick walls and tall Palladian windows betrayed its former incarnation as our town courthouse. "They didn't paint the woodwork," she said. "Again."

"Nope. Oh my God, look at Raven Meltzer," I said. "She got a tattoo."

Raven's a senior and the wildest girl in our school. She has dyed black hair, seven body piercings (that I can see, anyway), and now a circle of flames tattooed around her belly button. She's amazing to look at, at least for me—Ordinary Girl, with my long, all-one-length, medium brown hair. I have dark eyes and a nose that could kindly be described as "strong." Last year I grew four inches, so I'm five-six now. I have broad shoulders and no hips and am still waiting for the breast fairy to show up.

Raven headed to the side of the cafeteria building where the stoners hung out.

"Her mom must be so proud," I said cattily, but inside I admired her daring. What would it be like to care so little about what other people thought of you?

"I wonder what happens to her nose stud when she sneezes?" asked Bree, and I giggled.

Raven nodded to Ethan Sharp, who already looked wasted at eight-thirty in the morning. Chip Newton, who's absolutely brilliant in math, way better than me, and our school's most reliable dealer, gave Raven a soul handshake. Robbie Gurevitch, my best friend after Bree, looked up and smiled at her.

"God, it's so weird to see Mary K. here," said Bree, glancing around and running her fingers through her wind-tossed hair.

"Yeah. She'll fit right in," I said. My younger sister, Mary Kathleen, was headed toward the main building, laughing with a couple of her friends. Next to most of the freshmen, Mary K. looked mature and together, with grown-up curves. Stuff just comes easily to Mary K.—her hip but not-too-hip clothes, her naturally pretty face, her good but not perfect grades, her wide circle of friends. She's a genuinely nice person, and everyone adores her, even me. You can't help it with Mary K.

"Hey, baby," said Chris Holly loudly, coming up to Bree. "Hey, Morgan," he said to me. Chris leaned down and gave Bree a quick kiss, which she caught on her lips.

"Hey, Chris," I said. "Ready for school?"

"Now I am," he said, giving Bree a lustful smile.

"Bree! Chris!" Sharon Goodfine waved, gold bangles clinking on her wrist.

Chris grabbed Bree's hand and pulled her toward Sharon and the other usuals: Jenna Ruiz, Matt Adler, Justin Bartlett.

"Coming?" Bree asked, falling behind.

I made a wry face. "No, thank you."

"Morgan, they like you fine," Bree said under her breath, reading my mind as she often did. She'd dropped Chris's hand, waiting for me while he went on ahead.

"It's okay. I need to talk to Tamara, anyway." Bree knew I didn't feel comfortable with her clique.

She paused another moment. "Okay, see you in homeroom."

"See ya."

Bree began to turn away but stopped, her mouth dropping open like someone in Acting 101 doing "dumbstruck." I turned and followed her gaze and saw a boy coming up the steps to our school.

It was like in a movie when everything goes into soft focus, everyone becomes silent, and time slows down while you figure out what you're looking at. It was just like that, watching Cal Blaire come up the broad, worn front steps of Widow's Vale High.

I didn't know then that he was Cal Blaire, of course.

Bree turned back toward me, her eyes wide. "Who is *that?*" she mouthed.

I shook my head. Without thinking, I put my palm to my chest to slow my heartbeat.

The guy walked up to us with a calm confidence I envied.

I was aware of heads turning. He smiled at us. It was like the sun coming out of the clouds. "Is this the way to the vice principal's office?" he asked.

I've seen good-looking guys before. Bree's boyfriend, Chris, in fact, is really good-looking. But this guy was . . . *breathtaking*. Raggedy, black-brown hair looked as if he hacked at it himself. He had a perfect nose, beautiful olive skin, and riveting, ageless, gold-colored eyes. It took me a second to realize he was speaking to us.

I gazed at him stupidly, but Bree sparkled. "Right through there and to the left," she said, pointing to the nearest door. "It's unusual to transfer as a senior, isn't it?" she asked, studying the piece of paper he held out to her.

"Yeah," the guy said. He gave a half smile. "I'm Cal. Cal Blaire. My mom and I just moved here."

"I'm Bree Warren." Bree gestured to me. "And this is Morgan Rowlands."

I didn't move. I blinked a couple of times and tried to smile. "Hi," I finally said in a near whisper, feeling like a five-year-old. I'm never good at talking to guys, and this time I felt so overwhelmed and shy that I couldn't function at all. I felt like I was trying to stand up in a gale.

"Are you seniors?" Cal asked.

"Juniors," Bree said apologetically.

"Too bad," Cal said. "We won't have classes together."

"Actually, you might have some with Morgan," Bree said, with a cute, self-deprecating laugh. "She's taking senior math and science."

"Cool," Cal said, smiling at me. "I better check in. Nice meeting you. Thanks for your help." He turned and strode to the door.

"Bye!" Bree said brightly.

As soon as Cal passed through the wooden doors into the school building Bree grabbed my arm. "Morgan, that guy is a god!" she squealed. "He's going to school here! He'll be here all year!"

The next moment found us surrounded by Bree's friends.

"Who is he?" Sharon asked eagerly, her dark hair brushing her shoulders. Suzanne Herbert jostled her, trying to get closer to Bree.

"Is he going to school here?" Nell Norton asked.

"Is he straight?" Justin Bartlett wondered aloud. Justin's been out of the closet since seventh grade.

I glanced at Chris. He was frowning. As Bree's friends reviewed the meager info, I stepped back, out of the crowd. I drifted to the entrance and put my hand on the heavy brass handle, swearing I could still feel the warmth from Cal's touch.

A week passed. As usual, I felt a tingle in my chest as I walked into physics class and saw Cal there. He still looked like a miracle sitting in a dinged-up wooden desk. A god in a mortal place. Today he was focusing his beam on Alessandra Spotford. "It's like a harvest festival? Up in Kinderhook?" I heard him asking her.

Alessandra smiled and looked flustered. "It's not till October," she explained. "We get our pumpkins there every year." She tucked a curl behind her ear.

I sat down and opened my notebook. In one week Cal had become the most popular guy at my school. Forget popular; he was a celebrity. Even a lot of the boys liked him. Not Chris Holly or any other guy whose girlfriend was salivating over Cal, but most of the others.

"What about you, Morgan?" Cal asked, turning to me. "Have you been to the harvest festival?"

Casually I flipped to the current chapter in our textbook and nodded, feeling a rush of giddiness at hearing him say my name. "Pretty much everyone goes. There's not a lot else to do around here unless you go down to New York City, and that's two hours away."

Cal had spoken to me several times over the past week, and each time it had gotten a little easier for me to reply to him. We had physics and calculus together every day.

He turned in his desk to face me fully, and I permitted myself a quick glance at him. I don't always trust myself to do this. Not if I want my vocal cords to work. My throat tightened right on schedule.

What was it about Cal that made me feel like this? Well, he was gorgeous, for one obvious thing. But it was more than that. He was different than the other guys I knew. When he looked at me, he really looked at me. He wasn't glancing around the room, checking for his buds or trolling for prettier girls or sneaking quick looks at my breasts—not that I have any. He wasn't self-conscious at all, and he wasn't keeping score socially the way everybody else does. He seemed to look at me or Tamara, who was in advanced classes, too, with the same frank intensity and interest that he looked at Alessandra or Bree or one of the other local goddesses.

"So what do you do for fun the rest of the time?" he asked me.

I looked back down at my textbook. I wasn't used to this. Good-looking guys usually only talked to me when they wanted a homework assignment.

"I don't know," I said mildly. "Hang out. Talk to friends. Go to movies."

"What kind of movies do you like?" He leaned forward as if I were the most interesting person in the world and there was no one he would rather be talking to. His eyes never left my face.

I hesitated, feeling awkward and tongue-tied. "Anything. I like all kinds of movies."

"Really? Me too. You'll have to tell me which theaters to go to. I'm still learning my way around."

Before I could agree or disagree, he smiled at me and turned to face the front of the room as Dr. Gonzalez walked in, thumped his heavy briefcase on his desk, and began to call roll.

I wasn't the only person Cal was charming. He seemed to like everybody. He talked to everyone, sat by different people, didn't show favorites. I knew that at least four of Bree's friends were dying to go out with him, but I hadn't heard of any successes so far. I did know that Justin Bartlett had struck out.

2

I Wish

><"Beware the witch, for she will bind you with black magick, making you forget your home, your loved ones, yea, even your own face."
—WORDS OF PRUDENCE, Terrance Hope, 1723><

"You have to admit he's good-looking," Bree pressed, leaning against my kitchen counter.

"Of course I admit it. I'm not blind," I said, busily opening cans. It was my night to make dinner. The washed, cut-up chicken was sitting naked in a large Pyrex dish. I dumped out a can of cream of artichoke soup, a can of cream of celery soup, and a jar of marinated artichoke hearts. Voilà: dinner.

"But he seems like kind of a player," I continued mildly. "I mean, how many people has he gone out with in the last two weeks?"

"Three," said Tamara Pritchett, unfolding her long, skinny frame onto the bench in our breakfast nook. It was Monday afternoon, the beginning of the third week of school. I could safely say that Cal Blaire's arrival in the sleepy town of Widow's Vale was the most exciting thing that had happened since the Millhouse Theater burned to the ground two years ago. "Morgan, what *is* that?"

"Chicken Morgan," I said. "Delicious and nutritious." I reached into the fridge for a Diet Coke and popped the top. Ahhh.

"Toss me one of those," Robbie said, and I got him one. "How come when a guy dates a lot, he's a player, but if a girl does, she's just picky?"

"That is so not true," Bree protested.

"Hello, girls and Robbie," my dad said, wandering into the kitchen, his brown eyes somewhat vague behind his glasses. He was wearing his usual uniform: khaki pants; a button-down shirt, short sleeved because of the weather; and a white T-shirt underneath it. In the winter he wears the same thing except with a long-sleeved shirt and a knit sweater vest over it all.

"Hey, Mr. R.," Robbie said.

"Hi, Mr. Rowlands," Tamara said, and Bree waved.

Dad glanced around distractedly, as if to make sure that this was really his kitchen. With a smile at us he wandered out again. Bree and I shared a grin. We knew that soon he'd remember what he had come in to get, and he'd return for it. He works in research and development at IBM, and they think he's a genius. Around our house, he's more like a slow kindergartner. He can't keep his shoes tied, and he has no concept of time.

I stirred the mixture in the glass pan and covered it with foil. Then I grabbed four potatoes and scrubbed them in the sink.

"I'm glad my mom cooks," Tamara said. "Anyway, Cal has

gone out with Suzanne Herbert, Raven Meltzer, and Janice." She ticked off the names on her fingers.

"Janice Yutoh?" I squealed, putting the dish in the oven. "She didn't even tell me about it!" I frowned and added the potatoes. "God, he sure doesn't have a type, does he? It's like one from column A, one from column B, one from column C."

"That dog," said Robbie, pushing his glasses up on his nose.

Robbie was such a close friend, I hardly noticed it anymore, but he had terrible acne. He had been supercute until seventh grade, which made it all the harder on him.

Bree wrinkled her forehead. "The Janice Yutoh thing I can't figure out. Unless she was helping him with his homework."

"Janice is actually really pretty," I said. "She's just so shy, you don't notice it. *I* can't figure out Suzanne Herbert."

Bree almost choked. "Suzanne is gorgeous! She modeled for Hawaiian Tropic last year!"

I smiled at Bree. "She looks like Malibu Barbie, and she's got the brain to match." I ducked as Bree tossed a grape at me.

"Not everyone can be a National Merit Scholar," she said snippily. She paused and then said, "I guess none of us are wondering about Raven. She goes through guys like Kleenex."

"Oh, and *you* don't," I teased her, and was rewarded by another grape bouncing off my arm.

"Hey, Chris and I have been together for almost three months now," Bree said.

"And?" Robbie prompted her.

Self-righteousness mixed with rueful embarrassment crossed Bree's face. "He's bugging me a little," she admitted.

Tam and I laughed, and Robbie snorted.

"I guess you're just picky," Robbie said.

My dad wandered into the kitchen again, got a pen from the pen jar, and headed out again.

"Okay," Bree said, opening the back door. "I better get home before Chris freaks out." She made a face. "Where have you *been*?" she said in a deep-voiced imitation. She rolled her eyes and left, and moments later we heard her temperamental BMW, Breezy, take off and chug down the street.

"Poor Chris," Tamara said. Her curly brown hair was escaping from her headband, and she expertly twisted it back underneath.

"I think his days are numbered," Robbie said, taking a sip of soda.

I pulled out a bag of salad and ripped it open with my teeth. "Well, he lasted longer than usual."

Tam nodded. "It might be a record."

The back door flew open and my mom staggered in, her arms full of files, flyers, and real estate signs. Her jacket was wrinkled, and it had a coffee stain on one pocket. I grabbed the stuff from her hands and set it on the kitchen table.

"Mary, mother of God," my mom muttered. "What a day. Hi, Tamara, honey. Hey, Robbie. How have you two been? How's school so far?"

"Fine, thanks, Mrs. Rowlands," Robbie said.

"How about you?" Tamara asked. "You look like you've been working hard."

"You could say that," my mom said with a sigh. She hung her jacket on a hook by the door and headed to the cabinet to fix herself a whiskey sour from a mix.

"Well, we better head out," Tamara announced, picking up her backpack. She kicked Robbie's sneaker gently. "Come on, I'll give you a ride. Nice seeing you, Mrs. Rowlands."

"See you later," Robbie said.

"Bye, guys," my mom said, and the back door closed behind them. "Gosh, Robbie's getting tall. He's really growing into himself." She came over to give me a hug. "Hi, sweetheart. It smells great in here. Is it chicken Morgan?"

"Yep. With baked potatoes and frozen peas."

"Sounds perfect." She drank from her glass, which smelled sweet and citrusy.

"Tiny sip?" I asked.

"No, ma'am!" Mom replied, as she always did. "Let me change, and I'll set the table. Is Mary K. here?"

I nodded. "Upstairs with some of the Mary K. fan club."

Mom frowned. "Boys or girls?"

"I think both."

Mom nodded and headed upstairs, and I knew that the boys, at least, were about to get the boot.

"Hi. Can I sit here?" Janice asked at lunch period the next day, pointing to an empty spot on the grass of the school's courtyard next to Tamara.

"Of course," Tamara said, waving a handful of Fritos. "We'll be even more multiculti." Tamara was one of the very few African Americans in our overwhelmingly white school, and she wasn't afraid to joke about it, particularly with Janice, who was sometimes self-conscious about being one of very few Asians.

Janice sat down cross-legged with her tray balanced on her lap.

"Excuse me," I said pointedly. "Is there any interesting . . . news you'd like to share?"

Confusion crossed Janice's face as she chewed the school's version of meat loaf and swallowed. "What? You mean from class?"

"No," I said impatiently. "Romantic news." I raised my eyebrows.

Janice's pretty face turned pink. "Oh. You mean Cal?"

"Of course I mean Cal!" I practically exploded. "I can't believe you didn't say anything."

Janice shrugged. "We just went out once," she said. "Last weekend."

Tamara and I waited.

"Can you embellish, please?" I pressed after a minute. "I mean, we're your friends. You went out with the single best-looking guy on the planet. We deserve to know."

Janice looked pleased and embarrassed. "It didn't really seem like a date," she said finally. "It's more, like, he's trying to get to know people. Know the area. We drove around and talked a lot, and he wanted to know all about the town and the people...."

Tamara and I looked at each other.

"Hmmm," I said finally. "So you're not hooking up or any-thing?"

Tamara rolled her eyes. "Be blunt, why don't you, Morgan?"

Janice laughed. "It's fine," she said. "And no. No hooking up. I think we're just friends."

"Hmmm," I said again. "He *is* friendly, isn't he?"

"Speak of the devil," Tamara said softly.

I looked up to see Cal ambling toward us, his lips curved in a smile.

"Hey," he said, crouching on the grass next to us. "Am I interrupting anything?"

I shook my head and drank my soda in an attempt to look casual.

"Are you getting settled in?" Tamara asked. "Widow's Vale is pretty small, so it probably won't take you long to figure out where everything is."

Cal smiled at her, and I blinked at his supernatural face. By now I expected to have this reaction when I was around him, so it didn't bother me as much.

"Yeah. It's pretty here," Cal said. "Full of history. I feel like I've gone back in time." He looked down at a patch of grass, absently stroking a blade between his fingers. I tried not to stare, but I found myself wanting to touch what he touched.

"I came over to ask if you guys would come to a party this Saturday night," Cal said.

We were all so surprised that we didn't say anything for a second. It seemed gutsy for a relative stranger to throw a party so soon.

"Rowlands!" Bree called from across the lawn, then came and sank down gracefully on the grass next to me. She gave Cal a beautiful smile. "Hi, Cal."

"Hey. I've been going around inviting people to a party this Saturday," Cal said.

"A party!" Bree looked like this was the best idea she'd ever heard. "What kind of party? Where? Who's coming?"

Cal laughed, leaning back his head so I could see the strong column of his throat, with its smooth tan skin. In the vee of his shirt hung a worn leather string with a silver pendant dangling from it, a five-pointed star surrounded by a circle. I wondered what the symbol meant.

"If the weather's all right, it will be an outdoor party," Cal said. "Mostly I just want to have a chance to talk to people, you know, not at school. I'm asking most of the juniors and seniors—"

"Really?" Bree's lovely brows arched.

"Sure," Cal said. "The more the merrier. I figured we could meet up outside. The weather's been beautiful lately, and there's this field right at the edge of town over past Tower's market. I thought we could sit around and talk, look at the stars. . . ."

We all stared at him. Kids hung out at the mall. Kids hung out at the movie theater. Kids even hung out at the 7-Eleven when things got really slow. But nobody ever hung out in the middle of an empty field out past Tower's market.

"This isn't the kind of thing you usually do, is it?" he asked.

"Not really," Bree said carefully. "But it sounds great."

"Okay. Well, I'll print up some directions. Hope you guys can come." He stood smoothly, gracefully, the way an animal rises.

I wish he were mine.

I was shocked that my brain had formed the thought. I'd never felt that way about *anyone*. And Cal Blaire was so out of my league that wanting him seemed stupid, almost pathetic. I shook my head. This was pointless. I would just have to snap out of it.

When he was gone, my friends turned to one another excitedly.

"What kind of a party is this?" Tamara wondered out loud.

"I wonder if there'll be a keg or something," Bree said.

"I think I'm going out of town this weekend," Janice said, looking half disappointed, half relieved.

The four of us watched as Cal approached Bree's other

friends, who were hanging out on the benches at the edge of the school grounds. After talking to them, he headed to the stoners clustered by the doors to the cafeteria. The funny thing was, he looked just like each crowd he spoke to. When he was with the brains, like me and Tamara and Janice, he was totally believable as a gorgeous, brilliant, deeply inquisitive scholar type. When he was with Bree's friends, he looked cool, casual, and hip: a trendsetter. And when he was standing next to Raven and Chip, I could totally imagine him as a stoner, smoking pot every day after school. It was amazing how comfortable he was with everyone.

On one level I envied it since I'm comfortable with only a small group of people, my good friends. In fact, my two closest friends, Bree and Robbie, I've known since we were babies and our families lived on the same block. That was before Bree's family moved into a huge modern house with a view of the river and long before we'd split up into different cliques. Bree and I were two of the only people at our school who managed to be close despite belonging to different groups.

Cal was . . . universal, in a way. And even though I was nervous, I wanted to go to that party.

3

The Circle

><"Roam not at night, for sorcerers use all phases
of the moon for their craft. Be you safe at
home till the sun lights the sky and drives evil
to its lair again."

—Notes of a Servant of God,
Brother Paolo Frederico, 1693><

I am casting the net. Pray for my success, that I may
increase our number and find those for whom I search.

The porch light cast a shadow across our lawn. Before
me, on the crunchy, dried-out autumn grass, a smaller, darker
me walked to my car.

"What's wrong with Breezy?" I asked.

"She's making a weird pinging noise," Bree said.

I rolled my eyes, hoping she could see me. Bree's expensive, sensitive car was always doing one thing or another. So
much for fancy engineering.

I opened the driver's side door and eased onto the cool vinyl seat of Das Boot, my beautiful white '71 Chrysler Valiant. My dad likes to joke that my car weighs more than a submarine, so we named it Das Boot, the German word for *boat* and the title of my dad's all-time favorite movie. Bree climbed in the other side, and we waved good-bye to my dad, who was putting out the trash.

"Drive carefully, sweetheart," he called.

I started the engine and glanced out my window at the sky. The waning moon was a thin, sharp crescent. A wisp of a dark cloud drifted across it, blotting it from the sky and making the stars pop into prominence.

"Are you going to tell me where Chris is?" I asked as I turned onto Riverdale Drive.

Bree sighed. "I told him I'd promised to go with you," she said.

"Oh, jeez, don't tell me," I groaned. "I'm afraid of driving by myself at night; is that it?"

Bree rubbed her forehead. "Sorry," she muttered. "He's gotten so possessive. Why do guys always do that? You go out with them for a while, and suddenly they own you." She shivered, though it was barely chilly. "Turn right on Westwood."

Westwood headed right out of town, northward.

Bree waved the piece of paper that had the directions. "I wonder what this will be like. Cal is really . . . different, isn't he?"

"Uh-huh." I took a swig of seltzer, letting the conversation die. I was reluctant to talk to Bree about Cal, but I wasn't sure why.

"Okay, okay!" Bree said excitedly a few minutes later.

"This is it! Stop here!" She was already scrambling out of her seat belt, grabbing her macramé purse.

"Bree," I said politely, looking around. "We're in the middle of freaking *nowhere*."

Technically, of course, you're always somewhere. But this deserted road on the outskirts of town didn't feel like it. To the left were acres of cornfields, tall and awaiting harvest. To the right was a wide strip of unmowed field edged by thick woods that led back toward town in a large, ragged vee.

"It says to park under that tree," Bree instructed me. "Come on."

I eased Das Boot off the side of the road and glided heavily to a stop beneath a huge willow oak. That was when I saw moonlight glinting off at least seven other cars that hadn't been visible from the road.

Robbie's distinctive red VW Beetle sat glowing darkly like a giant ladybug under the tree, and I saw Matt Adler's white pickup, Sharon's SUV, and Tamara's dad's station wagon edged up neatly next to them. Parked in a sloppy circle around them were Raven Meltzer's battered black wreck, a gold Explorer that I recognized as Cal's, and a green minivan I thought belonged to Beth Nielson, Raven's best friend. I didn't see any people, but there was a somewhat trampled path through the tall, dried grass toward the woods.

"I guess we're supposed to go there," Bree said, sounding uncharacteristically unsure. I was glad she was here with me and that Chris wasn't. If I'd had to come by myself, I might not have had the nerve to show.

We followed the path of beaten grass, the cool evening breeze filtering through my hair. When we reached the edge of the woods, Bree pointed. I could barely make out the pale gleam of her finger in the forest darkness. Looking ahead, I saw it: a small clearing and shadowed shapes standing around a low fire ringed with stones. I heard low laughter and smelled the delicious scent of wood smoke coiling through the newly crisp air. Suddenly an outdoor party seemed like a brilliant idea.

We stepped carefully through the woods toward the fire. I heard Bree swearing under her breath—her chunky plat-form sandals weren't the best shoes for nighttime hiking. My own clogs were cheerfully crunching twigs underfoot. I heard a crashing sound behind us and startled, then saw it was Ethan Sharp and Alessandra Spotford, lurching through the forest after us.

"Watch it!" Alessandra hissed at Ethan. "That branch hit me right in the eye."

Bree and I emerged into the clearing. I saw Tamara and Robbie and even Ben Reggio from my Latin class. I went over to join the three of them as Bree split off from me to stand by Sharon, Suzanne, Jenna, and Matt. The firelight cast a soft golden glow on everyone's faces, making the girls look prettier than usual and the guys look older and mysterious.

"Where's Cal?" Bree asked, and Chris Holly straightened up from where he was crouched by an ice chest, a beer in his hand.

"Why do you want to know?" he said unpleasantly.

She ran her fingers through her hair. "He's our host."

Cal appeared almost silently from the edge of the clearing. He was carrying a large wicker hamper, which he set down next to the fire. "Hi," he said, looking around at us and smiling. "Thanks for coming. I hope the fire will keep you warm."

I pictured myself snuggling up to him, his arm around my

shoulders, feeling the heat of his skin slowly seep through my fleece vest. I blinked quickly, and the image was gone.

"I brought some stuff to eat and drink," Cal said, kneeling and opening his basket. "There's food in here—nuts, chips, corn bread. There's stuff to drink in the coolers."

"I should have brought some wine," Bree said, and I blinked in surprise to see her standing right there. Cal smiled at her, and I wondered if he thought she was beautiful.

For the next half hour we hung out and talked, sitting around the fire, maybe twenty of us altogether. Cal had brought some delicious apple cider spiced with cinnamon for people who didn't want beer, which included me.

Chris sat next to Bree, his arm around her shoulders. She wasn't looking at him but sent me irritated glances from time to time. Tamara and Ben and I sat with our knees touching. One of my arms was almost too warm from the fire, and the other was pleasantly chilly. From time to time Cal's voice flowed over me like the night air.

"I'm glad you all came tonight," Cal said, coming over to kneel next to me. He spoke loud enough for everyone to hear. "My mom knew people here before we moved, so she has a bunch of friends already, but I thought I'd have to celebrate Mabon by myself."

Bree smiled and leaned forward. "What's Mabon?"

"Tonight is Mabon," Cal said. "It's one of the Wiccan sab-bats. Kind of an important day if you practice Wicca. It's the autumnal equinox."

You could have heard a leaf land at that moment. We were all looking at him, his face golden and flame-colored, like a mask. Nobody said anything.

Cal seemed aware of our surprise, but he didn't look embarrassed or self-conscious. In fact, he plowed on. "See, usually on Mabon you have a special circle," Cal continued, crunching into an apple. "You give thanks for the harvest. And after Mabon you start looking forward to Samhain."

"Sowen?" Jenna Ruiz said faintly.

"*S-a-m-h-a-i-n,*" Cal clarified. "Pronounced Sow-en. Our biggest holiday, the witches' new year. October 31. Most people call it Halloween."

Silence, broken only by the crackling of the logs as they burned.

Chris was the first to speak. "So, what, man?" he said with a nervous laugh. "You saying you're a witch?"

"Well, yeah, actually. I practice a form of Wicca," Cal said.

"Isn't that like devil worship?" Alessandra asked, wrinkling her nose.

"No, no. Not at all," Cal responded in a way that wasn't the least bit defensive. "There is no devil in Wicca. It's about the tamest and most inclusive religion there is, truthfully. It's all about celebrating nature."

Alessandra looked skeptical.

"So, anyway, I was hoping to find a few people to make a circle with me tonight."

Silence.

Cal looked around, absorbing the surprise and discomfort in almost every face but showing no sign of regret. "Listen, it's not a big deal. Making a circle doesn't mean you're joining Wicca. It doesn't mean you're going against your religion or whatever. If you're not into it, don't worry about it. I just thought some people might think it's cool."

I looked at Tamara. Her dark brown eyes were wide. Bree

turned to me, and we shared a glance that communicated a whole conversation's worth of ideas. Yes, we were both surprised and a little skeptical, but we were both intrigued, too. Bree's look told me she was interested, she wanted to hear more. I felt the same way.

"What do you mean, a circle?" It was a few seconds before I recognized the voice as my own.

"We all stand in a circle," explained Cal, "and join hands, and give thanks to the Goddess and the God for the harvest. We celebrate the fertility of the spring and summer and look forward to the barrenness of winter. And we walk in a circle."

"You're joking," Todd Ellsworth said, sipping his beer.

Cal looked at him evenly. "No, I'm not. But if you're not into it, that's fine."

"Jesus, he's serious," Chris said to no one in particular.

Bree deliberately shrugged his arm off her shoulders, and he scowled at her.

"Anyway," Cal said, standing up. "It's almost ten. Anyone who wants to stay is welcome, but you're also welcome to leave. Thanks a lot for coming and hanging out, either way."

Raven stood up and walked over to Cal, her dark, heavily outlined eyes on his. "I'll stay." She turned a disdainful face to the rest of us, as if to say, "You wankers."

"I think I'm gonna go home," Tamara whispered to me, and stood up.

"I'm going to stay for a while," I said softly, and she nodded, waved good-bye to Cal, and left.

"I'm outta here," said Chris loudly, throwing his beer bottle into the woods. He got to his feet. "Bree? Come on."

"I came with Morgan," Bree said, moving closer to me. "I'll go home with her."

"Come on with me now," Chris insisted.

"No, thanks," Bree said, meeting my eyes. I gave her the slightest smile of encouragement.

Chris swore, then crashed off through the trees, muttering. I reached over and squeezed her arm.

I cast a glance at Cal. He was sitting with his knees bent and his elbows resting on them. There seemed to be no tension in his body. He just watched.

Raven, Bree, and I stayed. Ben Reggio left. Jenna stayed, so of course Matt stayed, too. Robbie stayed: good. Beth Nielson stayed, and so did Sharon Goodfine and Ethan Sharp. Alessandra hesitated but stayed, and so did Suzanne and Todd.

When it looked like everyone had left who was going to, there were thirteen of us standing there.

"Cool," Cal said, standing. "Thanks for staying. Let's get started."

4

Banishing

><"They dance skyclad beneath the blood moon in their unholy rites, and beware to any who bespy them, for you will turn to stone where you stand."

—WITCHES, WARLOCKS, AND MAGES,
Altus Polydarmus, 1618><

While we milled around uncertainly, Cal took a stick and drew a large, perfect circle in the ground around the fire. Before he joined the two ends of the circle, he gestured us inside, then closed the circle as if he were shutting a door. I felt a bit like a sheep inside a pen.

Then Cal took out a box of salt and sprinkled it all around the drawn circle. "With this salt, I purify our circle," he said.

Bree and I glanced at each other and smiled tentatively.

"Okay, now, let's join hands," Cal said, holding out his hands. A wave of shy self-consciousness washed over me as I realized I was standing closest to his left hand. He reached for my hand and held it. Raven went to Cal's other side, taking his right hand firmly.

Bree was on my other side, then Jenna and Matt, Beth, Alessandra, Todd, and Suzanne. Sharon, Ethan, and Robbie made up the other side, and Robbie held Raven's other hand.

Cal lifted my hand, and our arms were raised to the narrow patch of clear sky above us. "Thanks to the Goddess," Cal said in a strong voice. He looked around the circle at the rest of us. "Now you guys say it."

"Thanks to the Goddess," we said, though my voice was so low, I doubt I added anything. I wondered who the Goddess was.

"Thanks to the God," Cal said, and again we repeated it.

"Today day and night are balanced," Cal continued. "Today the sun enters the sign of Libra, the balance."

Todd chuckled, and Cal slanted his eyes at him.

I seemed to grow a billion extra nerve endings in my left hand. I tried not to think so much about whether I was holding Cal's hand too tightly or loosely, whether my hand was clammy from nervousness.

"Today the dark begins to dominate the light," Cal said. "Today is the autumn equinox. It's the time of harvest, when crops are gathered. We give thanks to the Earth Mother, who nourishes us." He looked around the circle again. "Now you guys say 'blessed be.'"

"Blessed be," we said. I was praying my hand didn't all out start sweating in Cal's. His was rough and strong, gripping mine as hard as possible without hurting it. Did my hand feel pathetically limp in return?

"It's the time to gather the seeds," Cal said in his calm

voice. "We gather the seeds to renew our crops for next year. The cycle of life continues to nourish us." He looked around the circle. "Now we all say 'blessed be.'"

"Blessed be," we said.

"We give thanks to the God, who will sacrifice himself in order to be reborn again," Cal said. I frowned, not liking the word *sacrifice*. He nodded at us.

"Blessed be," we said.

"Now let us breathe," Cal said. He bowed his head and closed his eyes, and one by one we did the same.

I heard Suzanne drawing in exaggerated-sounding breaths and opened my eyes a slit to see Todd smirking. Their reactions irritated me.

"Okay," Cal continued, opening his eyes after a few minutes. He seemed either unaware of or was deliberately ignoring Todd and Suzanne. "Now we're going to do a banishing chant, so we'll move widdershins—that means counterclockwise. You'll catch on."

Cal's body pushed me gently counterclockwise, and two seconds later we were all doing a Wiccan version of ring-around-a-rosy. Cal chanted, over and over so that we all learned it and could join in:

"Blessed be the Mother of All Things,
The Goddess of Life.
Blessed be the Father of All Things,
The God of Life.
Thanks be for all we have.
Thanks be for our new lives.
Blessed be."

It felt less weird after a couple of minutes, and soon I felt oddly exhilarated, practically running in a circle, holding hands under the moon. Bree looked so happy and alive that I couldn't help smiling at her.

A while later—it could have been two minutes or a half hour—I noticed I was starting to feel dizzy and strange. I'm one of those people who can never go on merry-go-rounds, roller coasters that do inversions, or anything that goes around in circles. It's an inner-ear thing, but the bottom line is I throw up. So I was starting to feel kind of iffy but didn't feel quite like I could stop.

Just as I was wondering what we would be banishing, Cal said, "Raven? What would you get rid of if you could? What do you banish?"

Raven smiled, and she looked almost pretty for a moment, like a regular girl. "I banish small minds!" she called gleefully.

"Jenna?" Cal asked as we moved in our circle.

"I banish hatred," Jenna said after a pause.

She glanced at Matt. "I banish jealousy," he said.

Holding tightly to Cal and Bree's hands, I raced in a circle around the fire, someplace between running and dancing, simultaneously pushed and pulled. I began to feel like a sliver of soap at the bottom of a bathtub whirlpool, going around and around, out of control. But I wasn't getting sucked toward the drain. Instead I was rising up through the ribbed circle of water, rising to the top, held in place by centrifugal force. I felt light-headed and weirdly happy.

"I banish anger," Robbie called out.

"I banish, like, school," Todd said.

What an idiot, I thought.

"I banish plaid golf pants!" said Alessandra, and Suzanne giggled.

"I banish fat-free hot dogs," Suzanne contributed. I felt Cal's hand tighten a bit around mine.

To my surprise, Sharon went next with, "I banish *stupidity*."

"I banish my stepmother!" Ethan yelled, laughing.

"I banish powerlessness," cried Beth.

Next to me Bree shouted, "I banish fear!"

Was it my turn? I thought dizzily.

Cal squeezed my hand hard. What was I afraid of? Right then, I couldn't remember any of my fears. I mean, I'm afraid of all kinds of things: failing tests, speaking in public, my parents dying, getting my period at school when I'm wearing white, but I couldn't think of how to phrase those fears to fit in with our banishment circle.

"Um," I said.

"Come on!" Raven cried, her voice tearing away, lost in the whirling circle.

"Come on," said Bree, her dark eyes on me.

"Come on," Cal whispered, as if he were enticing me into a private space with him alone.

"I banish limitations!" I blurted out, unsure where the words had sprung from or why they felt right.

Then it happened. As if obeying a director's cue, we threw our hands apart from one another, up in the air, and stopped where we stood. In the next instant I felt a piercing pain in my chest, as if my skin literally ripped open. I gasped, clutched my chest, and stumbled.

"What's with *her*?" I heard Raven say as I sank to my knees, pressing hard on the center of my chest. I felt dizzy, sick, and embarrassed.

"Too much brew," Todd suggested.

Bree's hand touched my shoulder. I sucked in breath and rose unsteadily to my feet. I was sweating and clammy, breathing hard, and felt like I was about to faint.

"Are you okay? What's the matter?" Bree put her arm around me and shielded me with her body. Thankfully I leaned into her. A cloudy mist swam before my eyes, turning everything around me into a heat mirage. I blinked and swallowed, wanting childishly to cry. With each breath I took, the pain in my chest was lessening. I became aware that the members of the circle were gathered around me. I felt their gazes on me.

"I'm okay," I said, my voice low and raspy. Heat came off Bree's tall, thin body in waves, and her dark hair was stuck to her forehead. My own hair hung around me in long, limp strands. Although I was sweating, I felt cold, chilled to the bone.

"Maybe I'm coming down with something," I said, trying to speak more strongly.

"Like witchitosis," Suzanne said sarcastically, her tanned face looking plastic in the moonlight.

I stood up straighter and realized the pain was almost gone. "I don't know what that was—a cramp or something." I broke away from Bree and tried a shaky step. And that was when I noticed something was wrong with my eyes.

I blinked several times and looked up at the sky. Everything was brighter, as if the moon had blown into fullness, but it was still just a sharp-edged crescent, a cream-colored sickle in the sky. I glanced at the woods and felt drawn into them, as if into a 3-D photograph. I saw every pine needle, every acorn, and every fallen twig in sharp relief. I closed my eyes and realized I could hear each separate sound of the night: insects, animals, birds, my friends' breathing, the delicate swoosh of my blood moving through my veins. The drone of crickets splintered into a thousand pieces—the music of a thousand separate beings.

I blinked again and looked at the faces around me, dim but utterly distinct in the firelight. Robbie and Bree wore expressions of concern, but it was Cal's face that held my eyes. Cal was gazing at me intently, his golden eyes seeming to strip through my skin to the bones underneath.

Abruptly I sat down on the ground. The earth was slightly damp and covered with a thin layer of decaying leaves. The crunching sound was incredibly loud in my ears as I tucked my legs beneath me. Instantly I felt better, as if the ground itself were absorbing my shaky feelings. I looked deeply into the fire, and the timeless, eternal dance of colors I saw there was so beautiful, I wanted to cry.

Cal's deep voice floated toward me as clearly as a whisper in a tunnel, as if his words were meant for me alone, and they found me unerringly even as the group dissolved into talking.

He said the words under his breath, his gaze fixed on my face. "I banish loneliness."

5

Headachy

><"A witch may be a woman or man. The feminine power is as fierce and terrifying as the masculine power, and both are to be feared."
—There Are Witches Among Us,
Susanna Gregg, 1917><

I saw something last night—a flash of power from an unexpected source. I can't jump to conclusions—I've been looking and waiting and watching for too long to make a mistake. But in my gut I feel she's here. She's here, and she has power. I need to get closer to her.

On Sunday morning I woke up feeling like my head was packed with wet sand. Mary K. stuck her head in my door.

"Better get up. Church."

My mom brushed past her into my room. "Get up, get up, you lazy pup," she said. She threw open my curtains, flooding my room with bright autumn sunlight that pierced my eye-balls and stung the back of my head.

"Ugh," I moaned, covering my face.

"Come on, we'll be late," said my mom. "Do you want waffles?"

I thought for a minute. "Sure."

"I'll put them in the toaster for you."

I sat up in bed, wondering if this was what a hangover felt like. It all came back to me, everything that had happened last night, and I felt a rush of excitement. Wicca. It had been strange and amazing. True, today I felt physically awful, foggy-headed and sore, but still, last night had been one of the most exciting times of my whole life. And Cal. He was . . . incredible. Unusual.

I thought back to the moment when he looked at me so intensely. I thought at the time he'd been talking to me alone, but I later realized he wasn't. Robbie had heard him banish loneliness, and Bree had, too. On the way home Bree had wondered aloud how a guy like Cal could possibly be lonely.

I swung my feet over to the chilly floor. It was really autumn, finally. My favorite time of year. The air is crisp; the leaves change color; the heat and exhaustion of summer are over. It's cozier.

When I stood up, I swayed a bit, then clawed my way to the shower. I stepped under the wimpy, water-saving shower-head and turned it to hot. As the water streamed down on my head, I closed my eyes and leaned against the shower wall, shivering with headachy delight. Then something shifted almost imperceptibly, and suddenly I could hear each and every drop of water, feel each sliding rivulet on my skin, each tiny hair on my arms being weighted down by wetness. I opened my eyes and breathed in the steamy air, feeling my headache drain away. I stayed there, seeing the universe in my shower, until I heard Mary K. banging on the door.

"I'll be out in a minute!" I said impatiently.

Fifteen minutes later I slid into the backseat of my dad's Volvo, my wet hair sleeked into a long braid and making a damp patch on the back of my dress. I struggled into my jacket.

"What time did you go to bed, Morgan? Didn't you get enough sleep last night?" my mom asked brightly. Everyone in my family except me is obnoxiously cheerful in the morning.

"I never get enough sleep." I moaned.

"Isn't it a beautiful morning?" my dad said. "When I got up, it was barely light. I drank my coffee on the back porch and watched the sun come up."

I popped the top off a Diet Coke and took a life-giving sip. My mom turned around and made a mom face. "Honey, you should drink some orange juice in the morning."

My dad chuckled. "That's our owl."

I'm a night owl, and they're larks. I drank my soda, trying to swig it all down before we got to church. I thought about how lucky my parents are to have Mary K. because otherwise it would seem as if *both* of their children were total aliens. And then I thought how lucky they are to have *me* so that they'll really appreciate Mary K. And then I thought how lucky I am to have *them* because I know they love me even though I'm so different from the three of them.

Our church is beautiful and almost 250 years old. It was one of the first Catholic churches in this area. The organist, Mrs. Lavender, was already playing when we walked in, and the smells of incense were as familiar and comforting to me as the smell of our laundry detergent.

As I passed through the huge wooden doors, the numbers 117, 45, and 89 entered my mind, as if someone had drawn them on the inside of my forehead. How weird, I thought. We sat down in our usual pew, with my mom between Mary K. and me so we wouldn't cut up, even though we're so old now that we wouldn't cut up, anyway. We know about everyone who goes to our church, and I liked seeing them every week, seeing them change, feeling like part of something bigger than just my family.

Mrs. Lavender began to play the first hymn, and we stood as the processional trailed in, the altar boys and the choir, Father Hotchkiss and Deacon Benes, Joey Markovich carrying the heavy gold cross.

Mom opened her hymnal and began flipping pages. I glanced at the hymn board at the front of the church to see what number we should be on. The first hymn was number 117. I glanced at the next number—45. Followed by 89. The same three numbers that had popped into my brain as I first entered the church. I turned to the correct page and began singing, wondering how I had known those numbers.

That Sunday, Father Hotchkiss gave a sermon in which he equated one's spiritual struggle with a football game. Father Hotchkiss is very big on football.

After church we stepped out in the bright sunlight again, and I blinked.

"Lunch at the Widow's Diner?" said Dad, as usual, and we all agreed, as usual. It was just another Sunday, except that for some reason I had known the numbers of the three hymns we would sing before I had seen them.

6

Practical Magick

><"They keep records of their deeds and write them in their books of shadows. No mere mortal can read their unnatural codes, for their words are for their kind alone."
—HIDDEN EVIL, Andrej Kwertowski, 1708 ><

I am not psychic. Life is packed with weird little coincidences. I'll just keep telling myself that until I believe it.

"Where are we going?" I asked. I had changed out of my Sunday dress into jeans and a sweatshirt. My headache was gone, and I felt fine.

"An occult bookstore," Bree said, adjusting her rearview mirror. "Cal told me about it last night, and it sounded great."

"Hey, speaking of occult, you know something weird?" I asked. "Today in church I knew the numbers for the hymns before I saw them on the board. Isn't that bizarre?"

"What do you mean, you knew them?" Bree asked, heading out of town on Westwood.

"These numbers just popped into my head for no reason, and then when we got into church, they were up on the board. They were our hymn numbers," I said.

"That *is* weird," said Bree, smiling. "Maybe you heard your mom mention them or something."

My mom is on the women's guild at church and sometimes changes the hymn numbers or polishes candlesticks or arranges the altar flowers.

I frowned, thinking back. "Maybe."

Within minutes we were in Red Kill, the next town to our north. When I was little, I had been afraid of going to Red Kill. The name itself seemed to be a warning of something awful that had happened there or would happen there. But actually, a lot of towns in the Hudson River Valley have the word *kill* in them—it's an old Dutch word meaning "river." *Red Kill* simply means "red river"—probably because the water was tinted from iron in the soil.

"I didn't know Red Kill had an occult bookstore. Do you think they'll have stuff about Wicca?" I asked.

"Yeah, Cal said they have a pretty good selection," Bree answered. "I just want to check it out. After last night I'm really curious about Wicca. I felt so great afterward, like I just did yoga or had a massage or something."

"It *was* really intense," I agreed. "But didn't you feel yucky this morning?"

"No." Bree looked at me. "You must be coming down with something. You looked awful on the way home from the circle last night."

"Thanks, how comforting," I said flatly.

Bree pushed my elbow playfully. "You know what I mean."

We sat in silence for a couple of minutes.

"Hey, do you have plans tonight?" I asked her. "My aunt Eileen's coming over for dinner."

"Yeah? With her new girlfriend?"

"I think so."

Bree and I wiggled our eyebrows at each other. My aunt Eileen, my mom's younger sister, is gay. She and her longtime partner had broken up two years ago, so we were all happy she was finally dating again.

"In that case, I can definitely make dinner," said Bree. "Look, here we are." She parked Breezy at an angle against the curb, and we got out, walking past the Sit 'n' Knit, Meyer's Pharmacy, Goodstall's Children's Shoes, and a Baskin-Robbins. At the end of the row of stores, Bree looked up and said, "This must be the place." She pushed against a heavy double-glass door.

Glancing down, I saw a five-pointed star within a circle painted on the sidewalk in purple—just like Cal's silver pendant. Gold lettering on the glass door said Practical Magick, Supplies for Life. I wondered about the odd spelling of the word magic.

I felt a bit like Alice about to go down the rabbit hole, knowing that simply entering this store would somehow start me on a journey whose ending I couldn't predict. And I found that idea irresistible. I took a deep breath and followed Bree inside.

The store was small and dim. Bree moved ahead, looking at things on the shelves while I hovered by the door and gave myself time to adjust after the bright autumn sunlight outside. The air was heavy with an unfamiliar incense, and I imagined that I could almost feel the coiling smoke brushing against me and winding around my legs.

After blinking a few times, I saw that the shop was long and narrow, with a very high ceiling. Wooden shelves that looked homemade lined the walls and divided the store into halves. The half I could see down was floor-to-ceiling books: old, leather-bound volumes, bright-covered modern paperbacks, cheesy pamphlets that looked like they had been photocopied at Kinko's and stapled by hand. I read some of the hand-lettered category signs: Magick, Tarot, History, Womancraft, Healing, Herbs, Rituals, Scrying . . . and within each category there were subcategories. It was all very orderly, though it didn't give that impression at first.

Just looking at the books' spines, I felt that my mind was blooming like a flower. I hadn't known books like this existed—ancient volumes describing magic and rituals. I was seeing a whole new world.

Bree wasn't in sight, so I walked down the aisle and headed for the other side of the store. She was looking at candles. One large shelf unit was like candle mania. There were huge pillar candles; tiny little birthday-style candles; candles in the shape of people, men and women; nice dining-table tapers; star-shaped votives: You name it, this store had it.

"Oh my God." I pointed to a candle in the shape of a life-size penis. At least I assumed it was life-size. I hadn't seen one up close since Robbie had flashed my class in first grade.

Bree giggled. "Let's get a bunch of these for tonight. They would make dinner really festive."

I laughed. "My mom would keel over."

Most of the other candles were pretty, hand dipped in graduating shades of color, some in earth tones, some in rainbow colors. A little rhyme came into my head: *Firelight, my soul is bright.* I didn't know where it came from—probably some Mother Goose book I had when I was younger. It reminded me of how I had felt the night before, looking into the fire at the circle.

"Are you looking for anything in particular?" I asked. Bree had moved to examine shelves of glass jars, each filled with herbs or powders. One section was called essential oils, with row after row of tiny dark brown glass vials. The air was heavy with scent there: jasmine, orange, patchouli, clove, cinnamon, rose.

"Not really," Bree said, reading jar labels. "Just checking it out."

"I think we should maybe get a book on the history of Wicca," I suggested. "For starters, anyway."

Bree looked at me. "You're getting into this, huh?"

I nodded self-consciously. "I think it's cool. I'm curious to learn more about it."

Bree smiled at me. "You're sure it's not just a crush on Cal?"

Before I could answer, she was studying a small bottle and opening it. The scent of roses after a summer rain filled the air.

I was about to say that wasn't it at all. Instead I stood there, staring at my clogs. I did have a crush on Cal. Though I knew better than anybody he was out of my league, I was drawn to him. What a pair we would make: Cal, the most beautiful person in the world, and Morgan, the girl who had never been on a date.

I stood still and silent in the aisle of Practical Magick, overwhelmed by a strange sense of longing. I longed for Cal, and I longed for . . . this. These books and these smells and these things. New emotions—passion; yearning; gnawing, inexplicable curiosity—were waking up inside me, and it was thrilling and threatening at the same time. One part of me wished they would go back to sleep.

I looked up to try to explain some of it to Bree, but now she was bent intently over the jewelry case, and I had no idea how to put my feelings into words.

As I was gazing blankly at the labels on the packets of incense, I felt a slight prickling on the back of my neck. I looked up and was startled by the intent gaze the store clerk had fastened on me.

The clerk was an older guy, maybe in his early thirties, but with short gray hair that made him appear older than he probably was. And he was looking at me with a focused, unmoving stare, as if I were a new kind of reptile, something incredibly interesting.

Most guys don't look at me that way. For one thing, I'm usually with either Bree or Mary K. Bree is straight-up gorgeous, and Mary K. is totally cute. I'd heard that a guy in my class, Bakker Blackburn, was thinking about asking her out. Already Mom and Dad had started instituting rules about dating and going steady and all that stuff—rules they hadn't needed to worry about with me.

I turned my back to the clerk. Had he mistaken me for someone he knew? Finally Bree came up and tapped me on the shoulder.

"Find anything interesting?"

"Yeah, this," I said, pointing to a package of incense called Love Me Tonight.

Bree smiled. "Ooh, baby."

Laughing, we headed for the bookshelves and started reading titles. There was a whole shelf of books labeled Books of Shadows. One by one I opened them, and they were all completely blank, like journals. Some were like cheap notebooks; some were fancier, with marbled endpapers and deckle-edged leaves; and some were bound in gold-stamped leather, oversize and heavy. I felt sudden distaste for the girlish, pink vinyl-covered journal I'd been keeping since ninth grade.

Fifteen minutes later Bree had chosen a couple of Wiccan reference books, and I had settled on one about a woman who had suddenly discovered Wicca when she was in her thirties and how it had changed her life. It seemed to explain Wicca in a personal way. The books were kind of expensive, and I don't have Bree's access to parental credit, so I was getting only one.

We headed to the counter.

"This it for you?" the store clerk asked Bree.

"Uh-huh." Bree dug in her purse for her wallet. "We can swap books when we're finished," she said to me.

"Good idea," I said.

"Do you have everything you need for Samhain?" the clerk asked.

"Samhain?" Bree looked up.

"One of the biggest Wiccan festivals," the clerk said and pointed to a poster tacked to the wall with rusty thumbtacks. It depicted a large purple wheel. At the top it said The Witches' Sabbats. At eight points around the wheel were the names of Wiccan celebrations and their dates. Mabon appeared at nine o'clock on the wheel. At about ten-thirty was the word *Samhain*, October 31. My eyes scanned the wheel, fascinated. Yule, Imbolc, Ostara, Beltane, Litha,

Lammas, Mabon, Samhain. The very words were strange and also somehow familiar and poetic-sounding to me.

Tapping it with his finger, the clerk said, "Get your black and orange candles now."

"Oh, right," Bree said, nodding.

"If you need more information, there are a couple of great books about our festivals, sabbats, and esbats," said the clerk. He was speaking to Bree but looking at me. I was dying for the books but didn't have enough money with me.

"Hang on—let me get them." Bree followed him back to the bookshelves to get the ones he recommended.

I heard a lightbulb flickering overhead and felt the spiral of incense smoke rising above its little stand. As I stood there, it seemed as if everything around me was actually vibrating, almost. As if it was full of energy, like a beehive. I blinked and shook my head. My hair suddenly felt heavy. I wished Cal were there.

The clerk returned while Bree continued browsing. He stared at me. The silence was so awkward I broke it. "Why is magic spelled with a K here?" I heard myself asking him

"To distinguish it from illusionary magic," he responded, as though it was very strange of me not to know this.

He went right back to his silent stare. "What's your name?" he finally asked me in a soft voice.

I looked at him. "Um, Morgan. Why?"

"I mean, who are you?" Though soft, the soft voice was quietly insistent.

Who am I? I frowned at him. What did he want me to say? "I'm a junior at Widow's Vale," I offered awkwardly.

The clerk looked puzzled, as if he were asking me a question in English and I was insisting on answering in Spanish.

Bree came back, holding a book called *Sabbats: Past and Present,* by Sarah Morningstar.

"I'll get this, too," she said, sliding it onto the counter. The clerk silently rang it up.

Then, as Bree took her paper bag, he said to me, "You might be interested in one of our history books." He reached for it beneath the worn wooden counter.

It's black, I thought, and he pulled out a black-covered paperback. Its title was *The Seven Great Clans: Origins of Witchcraft Examined.*

I stared at the book, tempted to blurt out, "That's mine!" But of course it wasn't mine—I had never seen it before. I wondered why it seemed so familiar.

"It's practically required reading," the clerk said, looking at me. "It's important to know about blood witches," he went on. "You never know when you might meet one."

I nodded quickly. "I'll take it," I said, and fished out my wallet. Buying it cleaned me out entirely.

When I had bought my books, we took our bags and stepped again into the sunny day. Bree slipped on her sunglasses and instantly looked like a celebrity going incognito.

"What a cool place, huh?"

"Very cool," I said, though for me that didn't express even a tiny part of the emotions storming in my chest.

7

Metamorphosis

>< "In many villages, innocents turn to their local witch as a healer, midwife, and sorceress. I say, better to submit to the will of God, for death must come to all in time."

—Mother Clare Michael,
from a letter to her niece, 1824 ><

I can't stop thinking about Practical Magick *and the strange mixture of fear and familiarity I felt there. Why did the names of the esbats and festivals feel like deeply buried memories? I never gave much thought to the possibility of past lives, but now, who knows?*

"Morgan! Mary K.!" my mom called from downstairs. "Eileen's here!"

I rolled off my bed, marked my place in the book, and put it on my desk next to my journal, trying to pull myself back into the regular world. I was blown away by what I had been reading—about Wicca's roots in pre-Christian Europe thousands and thousands of years ago.

My brain still felt glazed as I padded downstairs in my socks just as my dad came in the front door with bags of food from Kabob Palace, Widow's Vale's only Middle Eastern restaurant. The smell of falafel and hummus started bringing me back to my senses.

I went into the living room, where the rest of the group was already gathered.

"Hi, Aunt Eileen," I said, and hugged her hello.

"Hi, sweetie," she said. "I'd like you to meet my friend, Paula Steen."

Paula stood up as I turned toward her, a smile already on my face. The first impression I had was of animals, as if Paula were covered with animals. I stopped dead and blinked. I mean, I saw *Paula:* She was a bit taller than I am, with sandy hair down to her shoulders and wide, pale green eyes. But I also saw dogs and cats and birds and rabbits all around her. It was weird and scary, and I felt an instant of panic.

"Hi, Morgan," Paula said, her voice friendly. "Um, are you okay?"

"I'm seeing animals," I said faintly, wondering if I should sit down and put my head between my knees.

Paula laughed. "I guess I can never quite get all the fur off," she said matter-of-factly. "I'm a vet," she explained, "and I just came from a Sunday clinic." She looked down at her skirt and jacket. "I thought with enough masking tape, I might be presentable."

"Oh, you are!" I said, feeling stupid. "You look fine." I shook my head and blinked a couple of times, and all the weird afterimages were gone. "I don't know what's wrong with me."

"Maybe you're psychic," Paula suggested easily, as if she

were suggesting that maybe I was a vegetarian or a Democrat.

"Or maybe she's just a weirdo," Mary K. said brightly, and I aimed a kick at her leg.

The doorbell rang, and I ran to get it.

"What's she like?" whispered Bree, stepping into the foyer.

"*She's* great. *I'm* a freak," I whispered back as Bree hung her jacket on a peg.

"You can explain later," she said and followed me into the living room to meet Paula.

"Okay!" my mom announced a few minutes later. "Why don't you all come in and sit down? Food's ready."

Once we were seated and served, I thought back to what I had said. Why had I seen those images of animals? Why did I say anything?

In spite of my weirdness, dinner was great. I liked Paula right away. She was warm and funny and obviously crazy about Aunt Eileen. I was happy to have Bree there, talking to everyone and teasing Mary K. She felt like one of us, one of our family. Once she told me that she loves coming to our house for dinner because it feels like a real family. At her house it's usually just her and her dad. Or just her, eating alone.

As I was helping myself to more tabouli, I looked up and absently said, "Oh, Mom—it's Ms. Fiorello."

"What?" my mom asked, dipping her pita bread into some hummus. Just then the phone rang. Mom got up to answer it. She talked in the kitchen for a minute, then hung up and came to sit back down. She looked at me.

"It was Betty Fiorello," she said. "Had she told you she was going to call?"

I shook my head and applied myself to my tabouli.

Bree and Mary K. started humming the theme from *The X-Files.*

"She *is* psychic!" Aunt Eileen laughed. "Quick, who's going to win the play-offs for the World Series?"

I laughed self-consciously. "Sorry. Nothing's coming to me."

Dinner went on, and Mary K. teased me about my supernatural brain powers. A couple of times I felt my mother's eyes on me.

Maybe since I had been in the circle, since I had banished limitations, something inside me was opening up. I didn't know whether to feel glad or terrified. I wanted to talk to Bree about it, but she had to get home right after dinner.

"Bye, Mr. and Mrs. Rowlands," Bree said, putting on her jacket. "Thanks for dinner—it was great. Nice meeting you, Paula."

Later, after Aunt Eileen and Paula left, I went upstairs and did my calculus homework. I called Bree, but she was watching a football game with her dad and said she'd talk to me the next day.

Around eleven I got a weird urge to call Cal and tell him what was going on with me. Luckily I realized how completely insane this was and let the urge pass. I fell asleep with my face against the pages of *The Seven Great Clans.*

"Welcome to Rowlands Airlines," I intoned on Monday morning as Mary K. slid into the car, trying to hold her cardboard tray level so the scrambled eggs didn't slide into her lap. "Please fasten your seat belts and keep your seat in its upright and locked position."

Mary K. giggled and took a bite of her sausage patty. "Looks like rain," she said, chewing.

"I hope it does rain so Mr. Herndon won't clean his stupid gutters," I said, steering with my knees so I could open a soda.

Mary K. paused, her eyes narrowed. "Um, okaaay," she said in an exaggerated soothing tone. "I hope so, *too*." She continued chewing, giving me a sidelong glance. "Are we back to *The X-Files* again?"

I tried to laugh, but I was puzzled by my own words. The Herndons were an old couple who lived three houses down. I hardly ever thought about them.

"Maybe you're metamorphosing into a higher being," my sister suggested, opening a small carton of orange juice. She took a deep swig, then wiped her mouth on the back of her hand. Her straight, shiny, russet-colored hair swung in a perfect bell to her shoulders, and she looked pretty and feminine, like my mom.

"I'm already a superior being," I reminded her.

"I said higher, not superior," Mary K. said.

I took another drink and sighed, feeling my brain cells waking up. Another one of these and I would feel ready to face the day. Cal would be at school. Just the idea that I would see Cal soon, be able to talk to him, made me so pleasantly nervous that my hands tightened on the steering wheel.

"Um, Morgan?" Mary K.'s voice was tentative.

"Yeah?"

"Call me old-fashioned, but it's traditional to stop for red lights."

I snapped to attention, leaning forward, tensed to brake. Looking back quickly, I saw that I had just breezed through the intersection of St. Mary's and Dimson, right through a red light. At this hour of the morning there was always traffic. It was amazing we hadn't gotten into an accident—no one had even honked.

"Jeez, Mare, I'm sorry," I said, clutching the steering wheel. "I was daydreaming. Sorry. I'll be more careful."

"That would be good," she said calmly. She scooped up the last of her scrambled eggs and shoved the tray into my car's trash bag.

We managed to get to school without my killing us, and I found a great parking spot practically right outside the building. Mary K. was immediately surrounded by a gaggle of friends who ran over to greet her. Mary K. had arrived: The party could begin.

I saw Bree and Robbie hanging out not by the stoners, not by the nerds, not by the cool kids, but in a completely new area around the old cement benches that face each other across the brick path by the east-side door. Raven was there, Jenna and Matt, Beth, Ethan, Alessandra, Todd, Suzanne, Sharon, and Cal. Everyone who had done the circle Saturday night. My heart started a slow, dull pound.

Before I got there, Chris walked up and spoke to Bree. Frowning, she headed off with him, talking intently as they walked away.

"Hey, Morgan," said Tamara, walking up to me. I glanced over at Cal. He was talking to Ethan.

"Hi," I said. "How was your weekend?"

"Okay. I called you on Sunday, but I guess you were at church. How was the circle? What happened after I left?"

I grinned. "It was really neat," I said. "We just made a circle and went around the fire. We talked about things we wanted to get rid of."

"Like . . . pollution or what?" asked Tamara.

"Pollution!" I said. "That would have been a good one. I

wish I'd thought of it. No, stuff like anger and fear. Ethan tried to banish his stepmother."

Tamara laughed, and Janice walked up and joined us.

"Hi," she said, pushing her glasses up on her delicate nose. "Listen, Tam, I have to go put a proof up on Dr. Gonzalez's board. Want to come?"

"Sure," said Tamara. "Coming, Morgan?"

"No, that's okay," I said. They walked off, and I headed over to the east-side benches.

"Hey, Morgan," Jenna said, sounding friendly.

"Hi," I said.

"We're talking about our next circle," Raven said. "That is, if you've recovered." Today Raven was wearing a boned maroon corset, a black skirt, black ankle boots, and a black velvet jacket. Eye-catching.

I felt my cheeks heating up. "I'm recovered," I said, playing with the zipper of my hooded sweatshirt.

"It's not unusual for a sensitive person to have some kind of reaction to circles at first," said Cal in his low voice. The timbre of it fluttered in my chest. "I did myself."

"Ooh, sensitive Morgan," said Todd.

"So when's our next circle?" asked Suzanne, flicking back her surfer-blond hair.

Cal looked at her evenly. "I'm afraid you're not invited to our next circle," he said.

Suzanne looked shocked. "What?" she said, forcing a laugh.

"No," Cal continued. "Not you, nor Todd. Nor Alessandra."

The three of them stared at him, and I felt fiercely glad. I remembered how snide they had been on Saturday night. They were part of Bree's clique, and it was unthinkable that someone would stand up to them, would cut them out of something. I was enjoying it.

"What are you talking about?" Todd asked. "Didn't we do it right?" He sounded belligerent, as if trying to cover up embarrassment.

"No," Cal said calmly. "You didn't do it right." He offered no other explanation, and we all stood there, waiting to see what would happen next.

"I don't believe this," said Alessandra.

"I know," Cal said. He sounded almost sympathetic.

Todd, Alessandra, and Suzanne looked at each other, at Cal, and at the rest of us. No one said anything or asked them to stay. It was very odd.

"Huh," said Todd. "I guess we know when we're not wanted. Come on, ladies." He offered his arms to Alessandra and Suzanne, and they had no choice but to take them. They looked humiliated and angry, but they had brought it on themselves.

Daringly, I gave Cal a look of thanks, and he kept his eyes locked on mine for several beats. I couldn't look away.

Suddenly Cal pushed himself off the bench he'd been leaning against and came to stand in front of me. "What do I have behind my back?" he asked.

My brow creased for a second, then I said, "An apple. Green and red." It was as if I had seen it in his hand.

He smiled, and his expressive, gold-colored eyes crinkled at the edges. He brought his hand from around his back and handed me a hard, greenish red apple, with a leaf still attached to its stem.

Feeling awkward and shy, aware of everyone's eyes on me, I took the apple and bit it, hoping juice wouldn't run down my chin.

"Good guess," Raven said, sounding irritated. It occurred to me that she was probably jonesing for Cal big time.

"It wasn't a guess," Cal said softly, his eyes on me.

That afternoon when Mary K. and I got home, we found out that Mr. Herndon from down the street had fallen off a ladder while cleaning his gutters. He had broken his leg. Mary K. started calling me the Amazing Kreskin. I was so freaked out, I called Bree and asked if I could come over after dinner.

8

Cal and Bree

><"There exist Seven Houses of Witchery. They keep to themselves, marrying within their clans. Their children are most unnatural, with night-seeing eyes and inhuman powers."
—WITCHES, MAGES, AND WARLOCKS,
Altus Polydarmus, 1618 ><

There's a spark there. I wasn't wrong. I saw it again today. But she hasn't recognized it yet. I have to wait. She needs to be shown, but very carefully.

Bree answered the door. The night air was brisk, but I was comfy in my sweater.

"Come on in," she said. "Want something to drink? I've got coffee."

"Sounds good," I said, following her to the Warrens' huge, professional-style kitchen. Bree poured two tall mugs of coffee, then added milk and sugar.

"Your dad here?" I asked.

"Yep. Working," she said, stirring. "How unusual."

Mr. Warren is a lawyer. I don't get exactly what he does, but it's the kind of thing where he and a bunch of other lawyers defend big corporations from people who sue them. He makes tons of money but is hardly ever around, at least now that Bree's older.

Five years ago, when Bree was twelve and her brother, Ty, was eighteen, Bree's mom took off and divorced Bree's dad. It was a huge scandal here in Widow's Vale—Mrs. Warren moving to Europe to be with her much younger boyfriend. Bree's seen her mom only once since then and hardly ever talks about her.

Upstairs, in Bree's large bedroom, I dove right in. "I think I'm losing my mind. Do you think the circle was dangerous or something?" I sat nervously upright in her tan suede beanbag chair.

"What are you talking about?" Bree asked, leaning back against the pillows of her double bed. "All we did was dance around in a circle. How could it be dangerous?"

So I told Bree about my newly discovered sixth sense and that it had started after Saturday night. In a rush I told her how I had felt sick Sunday and saw animals around Paula. How I knew about Cal's apple and Mr. Herndon. I reminded her about Mom's phone call.

Bree waved her hand. "Well, if that stuff was happening to me, I might be a little weirded out, too. But I have to tell you—listening to you talk about it, it seems like you might be kind of overreacting," she said gently. "I mean, you might have heard your mom mention the hymn numbers. We already talked about that. Then the phone call—Ms. Fiorello calls your mom all the time, right? God, she's called every time I've been at your house! I can't explain seeing the animals—except maybe your subconscious picked up the scent of all the vet stuff somehow. And the other things—maybe it's just a bunch of weird coincidences all at the same time, so it adds up and freaks you out. But I don't think you're going crazy." She grinned. "At least, not yet."

I felt a little reassured.

"It's just that it's all at once," I explained, "and this whole Wicca thing. Have you been reading about it?"

"Uh-huh. So far I like it. It's all about women," Bree said, and laughed. "No wonder Cal is into it."

I smiled wryly. "Too bad for Justin Bartlett."

"Oh, Justin's dating someone from Seven Oaks," Bree said dismissively. "He can't hog Cal, too. Hey, remember all those Books of Shadows we saw at Practical Magick?"

"Uh-huh," I said.

"They're for witches," Bree said cheerfully. "Witches write down things in their Books of Shadows. Like a diary. They keep notes of spells and stuff they try. Isn't that cool?"

"Yeah," I agreed. "Do you think local witches go there to buy them?"

"Sure," said Bree.

I drank the coffee, hoping it wouldn't keep me up. "Do you think Cal keeps a Book of Shadows?" I asked. "With notes about our circles?" I was leading up to telling Bree about my feelings for Cal, but I was self-conscious. This was bigger and harder to explain than any shallow crush I'd ever had. And even though Bree had named it so casually in Practical Magick, she didn't know how much I liked Cal, how deep my feelings were.

"Ooh, I bet he does," Bree said with interest. "I'd love to see it. I can't wait for our next circle—I already know what I'm going to wear."

I laughed. "And how does Chris feel about this?"

Bree looked solemn for a moment. "It doesn't really matter. I'm going to break up with him."

"Really? That's too bad. You guys had so much fun over the summer." I felt a nervous flutter in my stomach and shifted back in the beanbag chair.

"Yeah, but number one, he's started being a jerk, bossing me around. I mean, screw that."

I nodded in agreement. "Number two?"

"He hates all this Wicca stuff, and I think it's cool. If he isn't going to be supportive of my interests, then who needs him?"

"Too true," I said, looking forward to having her around to hang out with more often, at least until she found his replacement.

"And number three . . . ," she said, twining her short hair around one finger.

"What?" I smiled and drained the last of my coffee.

"I'm totally and completely crazy about Cal Blaire," Bree announced.

For several long moments I sat there, encased by the beanbag. My face was frozen, and so was the breath in my lungs. So much for being the Amazing Kreskin. Why hadn't I seen this coming?

Slowly, slowly, I released my breath. Slowly I drew it in again. "Cal?" I asked, trying to sound calm. "Is that why you want to break up with Chris?"

"No, I told you—Chris is being an ass. I'd break up with him anyway," Bree said, her dark eyes shining in her beautiful face.

Inside my brain, nerve impulses were misfiring frantically, but a new thought managed to formulate. "Is that why *you* like Wicca?" I asked. "Because of Cal?"

"No, not really," Bree said thoughtfully, looking up at the paisley fabric on her bed's canopy. "I think I'd like Wicca even without Cal. But I'm just—falling for him in a big way. I want to be with him. And if we have this huge thing in common . . ." She shrugged. "Maybe it'll help us get together."

I opened my mouth, fearing that a thousand mean, angry, jealous, awful words were about to fly out. I shut it with a snap. So many pained thoughts were swirling in my head that I didn't know where to start. Was I hurt? Angry? Spiteful? This was *Bree*. My best friend for practically my whole life. We had both hated boys in fourth grade. We had both gotten our periods in sixth grade. We'd both had crushes on Hanson in eighth grade. We'd both sworn those crushes to eternal secrecy in ninth.

And now Bree was telling me she was crazy about the only guy I'd ever felt serious about. The only guy I'd ever wanted, even if I knew I couldn't have him.

I should have predicted it. My own feelings had blinded me. Cal is unmistakably gorgeous, and Bree falls in love easily. Obviously Bree would be attracted to him. Obviously Chris would be no competition for a guy like Cal.

Bree was so perfect. So was Cal. They would be awesome together. I felt like I was going to throw up.

"Hmmm," I murmured, my mind racing hysterically. I tried to take a sip from my empty mug. Cal and Bree. Cal and *Bree*.

"You don't approve?" she asked with raised eyebrows.

"Approve, disapprove, what does it matter?" I said, trying to hold my face in some normal position. "It just seems like he's gone out with a couple of different people already. And I think Raven's trying to get her claws into him, too. I don't want you to get hurt," I heard myself babbling.

Bree smiled at me. "Don't worry about me. I think I can handle him. In fact, I *want* to handle him," she joked. "All over."

The forced smile froze on my face. "Well, good luck."

"Thanks," Bree said. "I'll let you know what happens."

"Uh-huh. Um, thanks for listening to me," I said, getting to my feet. "I better get home. See you tomorrow."

I walked out of Bree's room, her house, stiffly and carefully, as if I were trying not to jostle a wound.

I started Das Boot's engine, then realized that chilly tears were sliding down my cheeks. Bree and Cal! Oh God. I would never, ever be with him, and she *would*. It was a physical pain inside my chest, and I cried all the way home.

9
Thirsty

><"Each of the Seven Houses has a name and a craft. An ordinary man has no hope against these witches: better to commend yourself to God than to engage in battle with the Seven Clans."
—THE SEVEN GREAT CLANS,
Thomas Mack, 1845 ><

Am I losing my mind? I'm changing, changing inside. My mind is expanding. I'm seeing in color now instead of black and white. My universe is moving outward at the speed of light. I'm scared.

The next day I woke early after thrashing unhappily all night. I'd had horribly vivid, realistic dreams, mostly featuring Cal—and Bree. I had kicked off my covers and was freezing now, so I grabbed them and burrowed under again, scared to go back to sleep.

Lying in bed, I watched my windows as they gradually grew lighter. I almost never saw this time of morning, and my parents were right: There was something magical about it. By six-thirty my parents were up. It was comforting to hear them moving in the kitchen, making coffee, shaking cereal into bowls. At seven Mary K. was in the shower.

I lay on my side and thought about things. Common sense told me Bree had much more of a chance with Cal than I did. I had no chance. I wasn't in Cal's league, and Bree was. Did I want Bree to be happy? Could I sort of live vicariously through Bree if she went out with Cal?

I groaned. How sick is *that*? I asked myself.

Was I okay with Bree and Cal going out? No. I would rather eat rats. But if I *wasn't* okay with it and they *did* get together (and there was no reason to assume they wouldn't), then it would mean losing Bree's friendship. And probably looking pretty stupid.

By the time my alarm went off for school, I had decided to perform the supreme sacrifice and never let Bree know how I felt about Cal, no matter what happened.

"Some people are coming over to my house on Saturday night," Cal said. "I thought we could do a circle again. It's not a holiday or anything. But it'd be cool for us to get together."

He was hunkered down in front of me, one tanned knee showing through the rip in his faded jeans. My butt was cold as I sat on the school's concrete steps, waiting for the classroom to open up for the math club meeting. As if in recognition of Mabon, last week's autumnal equinox, the air had suddenly acquired a deeper chill.

I let myself drift into his eyes. "Oh," I said, mesmerized by the minute striations of gold and brown circling his pupils.

On Tuesday, Bree had broken up with Chris, and he

hadn't taken it well. By Wednesday, Bree was sitting next to Cal at lunch, showing up at school early to talk to him, hanging out with him as much as she could. According to her, they hadn't kissed yet or anything, but she had hopes. It usually didn't take her very long.

Now it was Thursday, and Cal was talking to me.

"Please come," he said, and I felt like he was offering me something dangerous and forbidden. Other students walked past us in the thin afternoon light, glancing at us with curiosity.

"Um," I said in that stunningly articulate way I have. The truth was, I was dying to do another circle, to explore Wicca in person instead of just reading about it. I felt thirsty for it in a way that was unfamiliar to me.

On the other hand, if I went, I would see Bree go after Cal, right in front of me. Which would be worse, *seeing* her do it or *imagining* her doing it?

"Um, I guess I could," I said.

He smiled, and I literally, *literally* felt my heart flutter. "Don't sound so enthusiastic," he said. I watched in complete amazement as he picked up a strand of my hair that fell near my elbow and gently tugged on it. I know there are no nerve endings in hair, but at that moment I felt some. A hot flush rose from my neck to my forehead. Oh, Jesus, what a dweeb I am, I thought helplessly.

"I've been reading about Wicca," I blurted out to him. "I ... really like it."

"Yeah?" he said.

"Yeah. It just ... feels right ... in some way," I said, hesitating.

"Really? I'm glad to hear you say that. I was worried you would be scared off after the last circle." Cal settled next to me on the steps.

"No," I said eagerly, not wanting the conversation to end. "I mean, I felt crappy afterward, but I felt . . . alive, too. It was . . . like a revelation for me." I glanced up at him. "I can't explain it."

"You don't have to," he said softly. "I know what you mean."

"Are you—are you in a coven?"

"Not anymore," he said. "I left it behind when we moved. I'm hoping that if some people here are into it, we could form a new one."

I drew in a breath. "You mean, we could just . . . do that?"

Have you ever seen a god laugh? It makes you catch your breath and feel hopeful and shivery and excited all at the same time. That's how it was watching Cal.

"Well, not right away," he clarified with a smile. "Typically you have to study for a year and a day before you can ask to actually join a coven."

"A year and a day," I repeated. "And then you're . . . what? A witch? Or a warlock?" The names sounded overly dramatic, cartoony. I felt like we were conspirators, the way we were speaking softly, our heads bent toward each other. His silver pendant, which I now knew was a pentacle, a symbol of a witch's belief, dangled in the open vee of his shirt against his skin. Behind Cal, I saw Robbie enter the classroom where the math club was meeting. I would have to go in a minute.

"A witch," Cal said easily. "Even for men."

"Have you done that yet?" I asked. "Been initiated?" The words seemed to have a double meaning, and I prayed I wouldn't blush again.

He nodded. "When I was fourteen."

"Really?"

"Yeah. My mom presided. She's the high priestess of a coven, the Starlocket coven. So I had been studying and learning about it for years. Finally, when I was fourteen, I asked to do it. That was almost four years ago—I'll be eighteen next month."

"Your mom is a high priestess? Does she have a new coven here?" Outside, it was getting dark, and the temperature was dropping. Inside, the math club meeting had already started, and it would be warm and well lit. But Cal was out here.

"Yes," Cal said. "She's pretty famous among Wiccans, so she already knew a bunch of people here when we moved. I go to her circles sometimes, but they're mostly older people. Besides, part of being a witch is teaching others what you know."

"So you're actually a—witch," I said slowly, taking it in.

"Yep." Cal smiled again and stood up, holding out his hand. Awkwardly I let him pull me to my feet. "And who knows?" he said. "Maybe this time next year, you will be, too. And Raven and Robbie and anyone else, if they want."

Another smile and he was gone, and then it really was dark outside.

10

Fire

><"If a woman lies with a witch of the Seven Houses, she will bear no child except he wills it. If a man lies with a witch of the Seven Houses, she will bear no child."

—THE WAYS OF WITCHES,
Gunnar Thorvildsen, 1740 ><

Tonight I sent a message. Will you dream of me? Will you come to me?

"The movie is supposed to be great. Don't you want to see it? And Bakker's going to be there," Mary K. said. She came through the bathroom that connected our two rooms, pulling on her shirt. In front of my full-length mirror she turned, looking at herself from all angles. She gave her mirror image a big smile.

"I can't," I said, wondering why my fourteen-year-old sister had gotten not only her share of the family chest but my share, too, apparently. "I'm going to a party. Where are you all meeting?"

"At the theater," she said. "Jaycee's mom is driving us. Do you like Bakker? He's in your class."

"He's okay," I said. "He seems like a nice guy. Cute." I had a thought. "I heard he's been crushing on you. He's not being too—pushy, is he?"

"Uh-uh," Mary K. said confidently. "He's been really sweet." She turned to look at me as I stood in my underwear in front of my open closet. "Where's the party? What are you going to wear?"

"At Cal Blaire's house, and I don't know," I admitted.

"Ooh, that new senior," said Mary K., coming over to shove clothes around. "He is so hot. Everyone I know wants to go out with him. God, Morgan, your clothes really need help."

"Thank you," I said, and she laughed.

"Here, this is good," she said, pulling out a shirt. "You never wear this."

It was a dark olive green, thin, stretchy top that my other aunt, Margaret, had given me. Aunt Margaret is my mom's older sister. I love her, but she and Aunt Eileen haven't talked in years, ever since Eileen came out. Since Aunt Margaret had given me the sweater, I felt disloyal to Aunt Eileen when I wore it. Call me oversensitive.

"I hate that color," I said.

"No," Mary K. said emphatically. "It would be perfect with your eyes. Put it on. And wear your black leggings with it."

I scrambled into the shirt. Downstairs, the doorbell rang, and I heard Bree's voice. "Oh, no way," I protested. The shirt barely came down to my waist. "This isn't long enough. My ass will be hanging out."

"So let it," Mary K. advised. "You have a great ass."

"What?" Bree came in. "I heard that. That shirt looks great. Let's go."

Bree looked amazing, like a glowing topaz. Perfect, flyaway hair accentuated her eyes, making them striking. Her wide mouth was tinted a soft shade of brown, and she was almost quivering with energy and excitement. She wore a clingy brown velvet top that accentuated her boobs and low-slung drawstring pants. A good three inches of tight, flat stomach showed. Around her perfect belly button she had put a temporary tattoo of sun rays.

Next to her I felt like a two-by-four.

Mary K. shoved the leggings at me, and I put them on, no longer at all concerned about how I would look. A plaid flannel shirt of my dad's completed my ensemble and covered my butt. I brushed my hair while Bree tapped her feet with impatience.

"We can take Breezy," she said. "She's working again."

Minutes later I was sitting on a prewarmed leather seat as Bree stomped on the gas and flew down my street.

"What time do you have to be home?" she asked. "This may go till late." It was barely nine o'clock.

"My curfew's at one," I said. "But my folks will probably be asleep and won't know if I'm a little later. Or I could call them or something." Bree never has to call home and check with her dad about anything. Sometimes they seem more like roommates than father and daughter.

"Cool." Bree tapped her brown fingernails against the steering wheel, took a turn a bit too fast, and headed out Gallows Road to one of the older neighborhoods in Widow's Vale. Cal's neighborhood. She already knew the way.

*   *   *

Cal's house was awesome, huge, and made of stone. The wide front porch supported an upstairs balcony, and evergreen vines climbed up the columns to the second floor. The front garden was lush and beautifully landscaped and just on the verge of wildness. I thought of my dad humming as he pruned his rhododendrons every autumn and felt almost sad.

The wide wooden door opened in answer to our knock, and a woman stood there, dressed in a long linen dress the dark purple-blue of the night sky. It was elegant and simple and had probably cost a fortune.

"Welcome, girls," the woman said with a smile. "I'm Cal's mother, Selene Belltower."

Her voice was powerful and melodious, and I felt a tingling sense of expectation. When I got closer to her, I saw that Cal had inherited her coloring. Dark brown hair was swept carelessly back from her face. Wide, golden eyes slanted over high cheekbones. Her mouth was well shaped, her skin smooth and unlined. I wondered if she had been a model when she was younger.

"Let me guess—you must be Bree," she said, shaking Bree's hand. "And *you* must be Morgan." Her clear eyes met mine, her gaze seeming to pierce the back of my skull. I blinked and rubbed my forehead. I was actually physically uncomfortable. Then she smiled again, the pain went away, and she ushered us inside. "I'm so glad he's made new friends. It was hard for us to move, but my company offered me a promotion, and I couldn't say no."

I wanted to ask what her job was or find out what had happened to Cal's dad, but there was no way to ask without being rude.

"Cal's in his room. Third floor, at the top of the stairs,"

said Ms. Belltower, gesturing to the impressive carved staircase. "Some of the others are here already."

"Thanks," we both said a bit awkwardly as we climbed the dark, wooden staircase. Beneath our feet a thick flowered carpet cushioned our steps.

"She doesn't think it's weird to let a bunch of girls into her teenage son's bedroom?" I whispered, thinking about how my mom kicks boys out of Mary K.'s room at home.

Bree smiled at me, her eyes shining with excitement. "I guess she's cool," she whispered back. "Besides, there's a bunch of us."

Cal's room turned out to be the entire attic of the house. It went from front to back, side to side, and there were small windows everywhere: some square, some round, some clear, some made of stained glass. The roof itself was pitched steeply and rose to about nine feet in the center, only about three feet at the sides. The floor was dark, unpolished wood, the walls unpainted clapboards. In one small gable was an antique desk with school textbooks on it.

We dropped our jackets on a long wooden bench, and I kicked off my clogs, following Bree's example.

A small working fireplace was set into one wall. Its plain mantel was covered with cream-colored candles of various sizes, maybe thirty of them. Pillars of candles stood around the huge room, some on black wrought-iron stands, some on the floor, some atop glass blocks or even set on top of stacks of ancient-looking books. The room was lit only by candlelight, and the wavering shadows thrown on every wall were hypnotic and beautiful.

My eyes were caught by Cal's bed, standing off in a larger

alcove. I couldn't help staring at it, feeling frozen to the spot. It was a wide, low bed of dark wood, mahogany or even ebony, with four short bedposts. The mattress was a futon. The bedclothes were of plain, cream-colored linen, and the bed was unmade. As if he had just gotten out of it. Lit candles burned brightly on low tables at either side.

In the far alcove against the back wall of the house, bathed in shadows, the rest of the group was gathered. When Cal saw us, he came over.

"Morgan. Thanks for coming," he said in his confident, intimate way. "Bree, nice to have you back."

So Bree had been in his bedroom.

"Thanks for inviting me," I said stiffly, pulling my flannel shirt closer around me. Cal smiled and took both of our hands, leading us to the others. Robbie waved when he saw us. He was drinking dark grape juice from a wine goblet. Beth Nielson stood next to him, her hair newly bleached pale blond. She had medium brown skin, green eyes, and a short-cropped Afro that changed colors with her mood. Sometimes I thought of her looking like a lioness, while Raven looked like a panther. They made an interesting pair if they stood next to each other.

"Happy esbat," Robbie said, raising his glass.

"Happy esbat," Bree said. I knew from my reading that *esbat* was just another word for a gathering where magick was done.

Matt was sitting on a low velvet settee, with Jenna curled on his lap. They were talking to Sharon Goodfine, who was sitting stiffly on the floor, her arms around her knees. Was she here just for Cal, or had Wicca spoken to her somehow?

I had always thought of her as having it easy, with her ortho-
dontist father smoothing her path through life. She was full
figured and pretty and looked older than she was.

"Here." Cal handed Bree and me wineglasses of grape
juice. I took a sip.

A patchouli-scented breeze washed into the room, and
Raven arrived, followed by Ethan. Tonight Raven looked like a
hooker who specialized in S and M. A black leather dog collar circled her neck. It was connected by leather straps to a
black leather corset. Her pants looked like someone had
dipped her in a vat of shiny black spandex, and this was the
dried result. She wouldn't have stood out in New York City,
but here in Widow's Vale, I would have given money to see
her walk into the grocery store. Did Cal find this attractive?

Ethan looked like he always did: scruffy, with long, curly
hair, and stoned. It hadn't seemed odd to me that people
would have stayed the first time we did a circle—lots of kids
will try anything once. But it was interesting that everyone
except Todd, Alessandra, and Suzanne had come back, and it
made me look at them more closely, as if I were seeing all of
them for the first time.

This group had hung out a few times at school in a new,
multiclique assemblage, but here we separated into our old
patterns: Robbie and I together; Jenna, Matt, and Sharon together, with Bree going between me and them; Beth, Raven,
and Ethan together by the drinks.

"Good, I think everyone's here," Cal said. "Last week we
celebrated Mabon and did a banishing circle. This week I
thought we'd just have an informal circle and get to know
each other better. So, let's begin."

Cal picked up a piece of white chalk and drew a large

circle that almost filled this end of the attic. Jenna and Matt got up and pushed the sofa out of the way.

"This circle can be made out of anything," Cal said conversationally as he drew. On the floor were the smudged and faded outlines of other circles. I noticed that although he was drawing freehand, the end result was almost perfectly round and symmetrical, as it had been in the woods when he had drawn a circle in the dirt with a stick. "It can be a piece of rope, a circle of objects, like shells or tarot cards, even flowers. It represents the boundary of our magick energy."

We all stepped inside the chalk circle. Cal drew the circle closed, as he had done last week. What would happen if one of us stepped outside it?

Cal picked up a small brass bowl filled with something white. For a worried moment I thought it was cocaine or something, but he picked some up in his fingers and sprinkled it all around the circle.

"With this salt, I purify our circle," he said. I remembered he had sprinkled salt last time. Cal placed the bowl on the circle's line. "Placing this bowl here, in the north position, signifies one of the four elements: earth. Earth is feminine and nourishing."

In the last several days I had gone online and done some research. I had found out that there were lots of different sects of Wicca, as there are different sects of almost every religion. I had focused on the one that Cal had said he was a part of and had found more than a thousand Web sites.

Next Cal put an identical small brass bowl, filled with sand and a burning stick of incense, at the east side of the circle.

"This incense symbolizes air, another of the four elements," Cal said, focused but utterly relaxed. "Air is for the mind, the intellect. Communication."

In the south he stood a cream-colored pillar candle about eighteen inches high. "This candle represents fire, the third element," Cal explained, looking at me. "Fire is for transformation, success, and passion. It's a very strong element."

I felt uncomfortable under his gaze and looked down at the candle instead. Firelight, my soul is bright, I thought.

Finally, at the western side, Cal put a brass bowl filled with water. "Water is the last of the four elements," he said. "Water is for emotions. For love, beauty, and healing. Each of the four elements corresponds to astrological signs," Cal explained. "Gemini, Libra, and Aquarius are the air signs. The water signs are Cancer, Scorpio, and Pisces. Earth signs are Taurus, Virgo, and Capricorn. Aries, Leo, and Sagittarius are fire signs." Cal looked at me again.

Could he tell I was a fire sign—a Sagittarius?

"Now, let's join hands," he said.

I was closest to Robbie and Matt, so I took their hands. Robbie's hand was warm and comforting. It felt strange to be holding Matt's hand, smooth and cool. I remembered how Cal's had felt and wished I was standing next to him again. Instead he was sandwiched between Bree and Raven. I sighed.

"Let's close our eyes and focus our thoughts," said Cal, bowing his head. "Breathe in and out slowly, to the count of four. Let every thought still, every worry fade. There is no past, no future, only the here and now and we ten standing together." His voice was even and calm. I bowed my head and closed my eyes. I breathed in and out, thinking about candlelight and incense. It was very relaxing. Part of me was aware of everyone else in the room, their quiet breathing and the occasional shifting of their feet, and part of me felt very pure and removed, as if I were floating over this circle, watching it from above.

"Tonight we're going to do a purifying and focusing ritual," Cal explained. "Samhain, our new year, is coming up, and most witches do a lot of spiritual work to get ready."

Once again we moved in a circle together, holding hands, but this time we moved slowly in a clockwise direction—deasil, Cal called it, as opposed to widdershins, which is counterclockwise.

For a moment I felt nervous about the end of the ritual. The last time I had done this, I had felt like someone had buried an ax in my chest, then felt like crap for two days afterward. Would that happen again? I decided it didn't matter, that I wanted to try this. Then Cal began the chant.

"Water, cleanse us,

Air, purify us.

Fire, make us whole and pure.

Earth, center us."

We began to repeat his words. For several minutes or maybe longer we moved in a circle, chanting. Glancing around the circle, I saw people starting to relax, as if they felt lighthearted and happy. Even Ethan and Raven seemed lighter, younger, and less dark. Bree was watching Cal. Robbie had his eyes closed.

We began moving faster and chanting louder. It was right after this that I became aware of palpable energy building up around me, within the circle. I looked around quickly, startled. Cal, across the circle, met my eyes and smiled. Raven's eyes were closed now as she chanted and moved unerringly in our line. The others looked intense but not alarmed.

I felt pressed in upon somehow. As if a big, soft bubble were pressing in on me, all around me. My hair felt alive and crackling with energy, and when I next looked up at Cal, I gasped because I could see Cal's aura, glowing faintly around his head.

I was awestruck. A fuzzy band of pale red light was glowing around him, shimmering in the candlelight. When I glanced around the circle, I saw that everyone had one. Jenna's was silver. Matt's was green. Raven's was orange, and Robbie was surrounded by white. Bree had a pale orange light, Beth had a black one, Ethan's was brown, and Sharon's was pink, like her flushed cheeks. Did I have an aura? What color was it? What did this mean? I stared, marveling, feeling joyful and amazed.

As before, at some unseen signal the circle stopped abruptly and we all threw our hands into the air, our arms outstretched. My heart throbbed, and so did my head, but I didn't stumble or lose my balance. I just pulled in a fast breath and grimaced, rubbing my temples and hoping that no one noticed.

"Send the cleansing energy into yourselves!" Cal said firmly, making a fist and thumping it against his chest. Everyone did the same, and when I did, I felt a great warmth rush in and settle in my abdomen. I felt calm, peaceful, and alert. Immediately after that I became nauseated and sick. Oh, help, I thought.

Cal instantly crossed the circle and came over to me. I was swallowing hard, my eyes big, hoping I wouldn't be sick right there. I just wanted to cry.

"Sit down," Cal said softly, pushing on my shoulders. "Sit down right now."

I sat on the wooden floor, feeling motion sick and awful.

"What is it *this* time?" Raven said, and no one answered.

"Lean over," Cal said. I was sitting cross-legged, and he gently pushed on the back of my neck. "Touch your forehead to the floor," he instructed, and I did, rounding my back and flattening my hands, palms down. Instantly I felt better. As soon as my forehead touched the cool wood, with my hands braced on both sides of me, the waves of sickness passed, and I quit gasping.

"Are you okay?" Bree knelt next to me, rubbing my back. I felt Cal brush her hand away.

"Wait," he said. "Wait until she's grounded."

"What's wrong?" Jenna asked, concerned.

"She channeled too much energy," Cal said, keeping his hand on the base of my neck. "Like at Mabon. She's very, very sensitive; a real energy conduit."

After a minute or so he asked, "Better now?"

"Uh-huh," I said, slowly raising my head. I looked around, feeling embarrassed and vulnerable. But physically I was fine, no longer queasy or disoriented.

"Do you want to tell us what happened?" Cal asked gently. "What you saw?"

The idea of describing everyone's auras seemed intimidating—too personal. Besides, hadn't they seen them, too? I wasn't sure. "No," I said.

"Okay," he said, standing up. He smiled. "That was amazing, you-all. Thanks. Now, let's go swimming."

11

Water

>< "Nights of a full moon or the new moon are espe-
cially powerful for working magick."
—PRACTICAL LUNAR RITUALS,
Marek Hawksight, 1978 ><

"Oh, yeah," Bree said enthusiastically. "Swimming!"

"There's a pool out back," Cal said, crossing the room. He opened a wooden door set back into an alcove. Brisk night air swirled into the room, making some flames go out and others dance.

"Okay," Jenna said. "That sounds great."

Ethan looked hot, his forehead damp beneath the tightly curled ringlets on his head. He wiped his face on the sleeve of his army-surplus shirt. "Swimming would be cool."

Raven and Beth smiled at each other like the Siamese cats in *Lady and the Tramp,* then headed to the door. Robbie nodded at me and followed them. Bree was already through the door.

"Um, is this an outdoor pool?" I asked.

Cal smiled at me. "The water's heated. It'll be okay."

Of course, the huge thing going through my mind was that I hadn't brought a bathing suit, but somehow I felt if I mentioned this, everyone would laugh at me. I went through the door after Sharon, followed by Cal. Outside was a spiral staircase, and its steps led all the way down to the first floor, to the patio. I gripped the banister tightly and went down, hoping not to lose my balance.

Behind me I felt Cal's hand on my shoulder. "Okay?" he asked.

I nodded. "Uh-huh."

A cut-stone patio, pale in the moonlight, met the edge of the staircase. Outdoor furniture, covered with water-proof covers, looked like blocky ghosts. On the far side a bank of tall shrubs pruned into neat rectangular shapes separated the patio from the yard beyond. A doorway was cut into the shrubs, and Cal pointed to it.

I looked up at the sky, shivering without my jacket or shoes. The waxing moon looked like a bitten sugar cookie in the sky. Its light shone down, illuminating our path.

Through the hedge doorway was a pristine lawn of smooth, soft grass, not yet brown. It felt like velvet moss beneath my bare feet.

Beyond the lawn was the pool. It was classical in design, almost Greek looking. It was a simple rectangular shape, with no diving board, no metal handrail anywhere. At each end was a series of tall stone columns, grown over with vines that were starting to lose their summer leaves. To one side was a cabana with several doors, and I began to hope that maybe his family kept all kinds of bathing suits there for people to borrow.

Then I saw that Jenna and Matt were already shimmying out of their clothes, and my eyes opened wide. Oh, no, I thought. No way. I whirled to find Bree, only to see that she was behind me, in her bra and underwear, dropping her clothes neatly onto a chaise longue.

"Bree!" I hissed as she undid her bra. She pushed off her undies, looking like a beautiful, moonlit marble statue. Raven and Beth were undoing hooks and buttons for each other, laughing, their teeth white in the moonlight. Naked, they ran to the pool and jumped in, their jewelry jangling cheerfully.

Next Jenna and Matt slipped into the water, Matt following Jenna as she moved across the dark expanse. Jenna laughed and went under, then surfaced, sleeking back her hair. She looked timeless, almost pagan. Sweat broke out on my forehead. Please don't let this turn into an orgy or anything, I begged whoever was listening to my thoughts. I am *so* not ready for this.

"Relax," Cal said behind me. I heard the rustling of his clothes and willed myself not to faint. In another minute I would see him naked. Cal, naked. All of him. Oh my God. I wanted to see him but was also writhing inside with uncertainty. He put his hand on my shoulder, and I jumped about a foot in the air.

"Relax," he said again, turning me to face him. He had taken off his shirt but was still wearing his jeans. "It's not going to turn into an orgy."

I was startled by how accurately he had read my thoughts.

"I wasn't worried about that," I said, appalled to hear a faint tremble in my voice. "It's just ... I catch cold easily."

He laughed and started undoing his jeans. My breath got stuck in my throat. "You won't catch cold," he said.

He pushed down his jeans, and I spun to face the swimming pool. I was rewarded by the sight of a naked Robbie walking down the broad steps into the water. What next?

Ethan was sitting on a chaise, peeling off his socks. His shirt was off, a lit cigarette dangled from his mouth, and his fatigue pants were unbuttoned and partially unzipped. He took a last drag on his cigarette and stubbed it out on the ground. Then he stood and dropped his pants as Bree and Sharon walked past him to the pool. His eyes narrowed and locked on their bodies, then he kicked off his pants and followed them. At the deep end he jumped in cleanly, and I prayed he knew how to swim and wasn't so stoned he would drown.

Raven and Beth were splashing each other, then Beth squealed and jumped, her dark body sleek and sparkling with water drops. Ethan surfaced close by, grinning like a fox. With his hair wet and off his face and out of his sloppy clothes, he was cuter than usual, and Sharon looked at him in surprise, as if wondering who he was.

Cal walked past me. "Come on, Morgan," he said, holding out his hand. He was completely starkers, and my cheeks turned to fire as I tried not to look down.

"I can't," I whispered, hoping no one else could hear me. I felt like such a sissy. I glanced over to the pool and saw Bree watching us. I gave her a weak smile, and she smiled back, her eyes on Cal.

He waited. If he and I had been alone, I might have gotten over myself. Maybe I could have taken off my clothes and prayed he wasn't a boob man. But every girl here was prettier than I was and had a better body. Every one of them had bigger breasts than me. Sharon's were humongous.

I needed an out. I was overwhelmed to begin with, and this was just too much.

"Please come swimming," Cal said. "No one will attack you. I promise."

"It isn't that," I muttered. I wanted to look at him, but I couldn't look at him with him looking at me. A storm of self-consciousness raged inside me.

"There are a lot of special aspects to water," Cal said patiently. "Being surrounded by water, especially under the moon, can be very magickal, a very special kind of energy. I want you to feel that. Just wear your bra and underwear."

"I don't wear a bra," I said, then instantly wanted to kick myself.

He grinned. "Really."

"I don't exactly need to," I mumbled unhappily.

He cocked his head, still grinning. "Really," he said.

I panicked, my breaking point reached.

"I have to get home. Thanks for the circle," I said, turning to go. I had come here in Bree's car, so I figured I had a long, chilly walk ahead of me. To go from the wonder and amazement of the circle to this painful humiliation seemed too much to bear. I couldn't wait till I was home, in my own bed.

Then Cal's hand snaked out and gripped the back of my shirt. With a gentle tug he drew me toward him. I wasn't breathing or thinking anymore. He bent over, put an arm under my knees, and picked me up. Strangely, I remember not feeling heavy or clumsy, but light and small in his arms. I stopped processing sensations in any normal way. I stopped being aware of the other people nearby.

He walked steadily down the pool steps into the shallow end. I didn't protest; I didn't say anything at all. I don't know if I could have. Then we were surrounded by water the exact temperature of my blood, and we were in the water, pressed together under the moon.

It was terrifying, strange, mysterious, thrilling, crushing.

And it was magickal.

12
What Goes Around

><"Should you be caught amidst two warring clans,
lie belly to earth and say your prayers."
—Old Scottish saying ><

When I got home from church the next day, Bree was sitting on our front steps, looking chilly and pissed.

I'd caught a ride home with Beth the night before because I had a curfew and Bree didn't. But I knew from the stony looks Bree gave me as I hurried from Cal's house that this was coming.

We went inside and up to my room.

"I thought you were my friend," she hissed as soon as the door was shut.

I didn't pretend not to know what she was talking about. "Of course I'm your friend," I said, unbuttoning the dress I had worn to church.

"Then explain last night to me," she said, her dark eyes narrowed. She crossed her arms over her chest and dropped onto the edge of my bed. "You and Cal, in the swimming pool."

I pulled a shirt over my head, then grabbed some socks out of my drawer. "I don't know *how* to explain it," I said. "I mean, I know you like Cal. I know I'm not competition for you. I didn't do anything. I mean, God, as soon as I could stand up in the water, he put me down." I tugged on my socks and slithered into my oldest, most comfortable jeans, automatically turning them up an inch on the bottoms.

"Well, what was the big coy act about before that? Were you playing hard to get? Were you hoping he would just rip your clothes off?" There was a sneer in her voice that stung, and I felt the first threads of anger rising in me.

"Of course not!" I snapped. "If he had ripped my clothes off, I would have run home screaming and called the cops. Don't be an idiot."

Bree stood up and jabbed her finger at me. "Don't *you* be an idiot!" she said. I had never seen her like this. "You know I'm in love with him!" Bree said, her face furious. "I don't just *like* him! I *love* him. And I want him. And I want *you* to leave him alone!"

"Fine!" I practically yelled. I stood and spread my arms wide. "But I wasn't doing anything, and I can't control what *he* does! Maybe he's just paying attention to me because he wants me to be a witch." As soon as I said that, Bree and I stared at each other. In my heart, I suddenly felt it was true. Bree's brow wrinkled as she thought back through the night before.

"Look," I said more calmly. "I don't know what he's doing.

For all I know, he has another girlfriend somewhere, or maybe Raven has already gotten to him. But I do know that *I* am not coming on to *him*. That's all I can tell you. And that'll have to be good enough." I pulled my hair over my shoulder and started to braid it with quick, practiced motions.

Bree glared at me for another moment, and then her face crumpled and she sank down on my bed. "Okay," she said, sounding like she was trying not to cry. "You're right. I'm sorry. You weren't doing anything. I was just jealous, that's all." She put her hands over her face and leaned down against my pillows. "When I saw him holding you, I just went crazy. I've never wanted anyone this bad before, and I've been working on him all week, and he doesn't seem to notice me."

I was still angry, but perversely, I also felt sorry for her. "Bree," I said, sitting down in my desk chair. "Cal left his coven behind when he moved, and he's hoping some of us will help him start a new coven. He knows I'm interested in Wicca, and I guess he thinks it's, I don't know, interesting or something that I have such a strong reaction to circles. Maybe he thinks I could be a good witch, and that's what he wants."

Bree looked up, her eyes filled with tears. "Do you really have a strong reaction to circles, or are you just pretending to?" she asked, her voice wobbly.

My eyes almost popped out of my head. "Bree! For God's sake! Why would I pretend that? It's embarrassing and un-comfortable." I shook my head. "It's like you don't even *know* me or something. But to answer your question," I said tersely, "no, I'm not *pretending* to have a strong reaction."

Bree covered her face with her hands and started crying. "I'm sorry," she sobbed. "I didn't mean that. I know you aren't pretending. I don't know what I'm doing." She stood up and grabbed a tissue from the box, then came over and hugged me. It was hard for me to hug her back, but in the end of course I did. "I'm sorry," she said again, crying against me. "I'm sorry, Morgan."

We stood there with her crying for a few minutes, and I felt like crying myself. Have you ever been afraid to start crying because you weren't sure if you'd be able to stop? That's how I felt. To fight with Bree about anything was horrible. To want Cal and not ever be able to have him made me feel desperate. For my best friend to want the same guy I did was a nightmare. To discover the complicated world of Wicca and feel drawn to it was confusing and almost scary.

Finally Bree's crying quieted, and she disentangled herself from me, wiping her nose and eyes. "I'm so sorry," she whispered. "Do you forgive me?"

I hesitated only a moment, then nodded. I mean, I love Bree. After my family, I love her the best in the world. I sighed, and we moved over to sit on my narrow bed.

"Look," I said. "Last night I didn't want to take off my clothes because—I'm shy. I admit it, okay? I'm a total wuss. You couldn't pay me enough money to stand naked next to you and those other girls."

Bree sniffled and turned to look at me. "What are you talking about?"

"Bree, please," I said. "I know what I look like. I have a mirror. I'm not a total woofer, but I'm not you. I'm not Jenna. I'm not even Mary K."

"You look fine," Bree said, frowning.

I rolled my eyes. "Bree. I'm pretty plain. And surely you've noticed that somehow nature has forgotten to give me any kind of bazongas."

Bree's dark eyes glanced quickly to my chest, and I crossed my arms.

"No, you're just, you know," Bree said lamely.

"I just am completely and totally flat chested," I said. "So if you think I'm going to go prancing around naked with you, Miss 36C, Jenna, Raven, Beth, and Miss January Sharon Goodfine, you are out of your mind. And in front of guys, people we go to school with! Give me a break! Like I really want Ethan Sharp to know what I look like naked. Jesus! No way!"

"Don't take the Lord's name in vain," Mary K. said, poking her head through the bathroom door. "Who were you prancing around naked with?"

"Oh, crap, Mary K.!" I said. "I didn't know you were there!"

She smirked at me. "Obviously. Now, who were you prancing around naked with? Can I go next time? I like my body."

I started laughing and threw a pillow at her. Bree was laughing, too, and I was relieved to see that our fight appeared to be over.

"You are not getting naked anywhere," I said, trying to sound stern. "You're fourteen years old, no matter what Bakker Blackburn thinks."

"Are you dating Bakker?" Bree asked. "I went out with him."

"Really?" said Mary K.

"Oh, that's right," I said. "I forgot."

"We went out a couple of times freshman year," Bree said. She sat up and stretched, arching her back.

"What happened?" Mary K. asked.

"I dumped him," said Bree without remorse. "Ranjit asked

me out, and I said yes. Ranjit has the most beautiful eyes."

"Then Ranjit dumped you to go out with Leslie Raines," I said, the whole story coming back to me. "They're still going out."

Bree shrugged. "What goes around comes around."

Which, of course, is one of the most basic Wiccan tenets.

13

Stirring

> ⋈"If you look, you will see the mark of a House on
> its progeny. These marks take many forms, but a
> trained witchfinder can always discover one."
> —NOTES OF A SERVANT OF GOD,
> Brother Paolo Frederico, 1693⋈

*I don't understand my mother at all. It's not as if I've done
something wrong. I hope she calms down. She has to, she
just has to.*

On Monday afternoon I skipped chess club and drove to
Red Kill, to Practical Magick. As I drove, I soaked up my
favorite signs of autumn: trees streaked with bright, vivid colors, protesting the little death of winter. Tall roadside grasses
were feathery and tan. Small farmers' stands sold pumpkins,
late corn, squash, apples, apple pies.

In Red Kill, I found a parking spot right in front of the
store. Inside, it was again dim and full of the rich smells of

herbs, oils, and incense. I breathed deeply as my eyes adjusted to the light. This time there were more customers than the last time.

I worked my way down the rows of books, looking for a general history of Wicca. Last night I had finished my book on the Seven Great Clans, and I was hungry for more information.

The first person I ran into was Paula Steen, my aunt's new girlfriend. She was crouched on the floor, examining books along the bottom shelf. Paula looked up, saw me, recognized me, and smiled. "Morgan!" she said, standing up. "Fancy meeting you here. How are you?"

"Oh, okay," I said, making myself smile back. "How are you?"

I liked Paula a lot, but this was a weird place to run into her, and I felt slightly nervous about it. She would mention it to Aunt Eileen, and Aunt Eileen would tell my mom. I wasn't keeping anything secret from my parents, exactly, but I hadn't gone out of my way to tell them about the circles or Cal or Wicca, either.

"Fine," she said. "Overworked, as usual. Today one of my surgery patients canceled, so I played hooky and came here." She looked around the store. "I love this place. They have all kinds of neat stuff."

"Yeah," I said. "Are you . . . into Wicca?"

"No, not me." Paula laughed. "I know lots of people who are, though. It's so pro-woman, it's sometimes popular with lesbians. But I'm still Jewish. I'm here looking at homeopathic books about animal medicine. I just went to a conference where they taught a course on pet massage, and I'm looking for more information."

"Really?" I grinned. "You mean, like giving your German shepherd a rubdown?"

Paula laughed again. "Kind of," she said. "Just like with people, there's a lot to be said for the healing touch."

"Cool," I said.

"Anyway, how about you? Are you into Wicca?"

"Well . . . I'm curious about it," I said in a measured tone, not wanting to blurt out all my messy feelings. "I'm Catholic and everything, like my parents," I went on in a rush. "But I do think Wicca is . . . interesting."

"Like anything else, it's what you bring to it," Paula said.

"Yes," I agreed. "That's true."

"Okay, I better run, Morgan. Good seeing you again."

"You too. Tell Aunt Eileen I said hi."

Paula took her books and checked out, and I examined the shelves again. I found a book that offered a broad general history and also explained the differences between some of the different branches of Wicca: Pecti-Wita, Caledonii, Celtic, Teutonic, Strega, and others I had learned about on the Internet. Tucking it under my arm, I looked through the stuff on the other side: the incense, the mortars and pestles, the candles separated by color. I saw one candle that was in the shape of a man and a woman joined, and it made me think first of me and Cal. Then my mind jumped to Bree and Cal. If I burned that candle, would Cal be mine? What would Bree do?

It was stupid even thinking about it.

I got in line, the scents of cinnamon and nutmeg all around me.

"Why, Morgan, dear, is that you?"

I whirled to find myself looking into the face of Mrs.

Petrie, a woman from my church. "Hi, Mrs. Petrie," I said a bit stiffly. What a strange run of luck. Somehow I'd expected more privacy on my little adventure this afternoon.

Mrs. Petrie was shorter than me now but hadn't changed in looks for as long as I could remember. She always wore tidy two-piece suits, stockings, and matching shoes. In church she wore matching hats.

Now she read my book's title. "You must be doing research for a school project," she said, smiling.

"Yes," I said, nodding. "We're studying different religions of the world."

"How interesting." She leaned closer to me and lowered her voice. "This is a very unique bookstore. Some of the things in here are awful, but the people who run it are very nice."

"Oh," I said. "Um, why are you here?"

Mrs. Petrie motioned over at the spices-and-herbs wall. "You know I'm famous for my herb garden," she said proudly. "I'm one of their suppliers. I also grow herbs for some of the restaurants in town and for Nature's Way, the health food store on Main."

"Oh, really? I didn't know that," I said blankly.

"Yes," she said. "I was just dropping off some dried thyme and some of last summer's caraway seeds. Now I must run. Good seeing you, dear. Tell your parents hello."

"Sure will," I said. "See you Sunday." Yes, indeed. I was relieved when she disappeared through the door.

I was so preoccupied with unexpected encounters that I had forgotten how oddly the clerk had behaved last time. But as I pushed my books across the counter, I felt his eyes on me again.

Wordlessly I took out my wallet and counted money.

"I thought you'd be back," he said softly, ringing up my books.

I stood stone-faced, not looking at him.

"You have the mark of the Goddess on you," he said. "Do you know your clan?"

My eyes flew to his, startled. "I'm not from any clan," I said.

The clerk cocked his head thoughtfully. "Are you sure?"

He handed me my change, and I took it, then grabbed my book and got out of there. As I cranked Das Boot's big, V-8 engine, I thought about the Seven Great Clans. Over the last few hundred years they had been disbanded and hardly existed anymore. I shook my head. The only clan I was a part of was the Rowlands clan, no matter what the clerk thought.

I took the small roads home and let the fiery leaves blur into the background as I sank into the daydream I was indulging in more and more often: the cherished moment, under the moon, when Cal carried me into the water. Fantasy and memory ran together, and I wasn't even sure it had actually happened anymore.

That night Mary K. made dinner, and it was my turn to clean up. I stood at the sink, rinsing plates, daydreaming about Cal, wondering if Bree and Cal had gotten together today after school. Had they kissed yet? It made my chest feel tight, and I commanded my mind not to torture me anymore.

Why had Cal come into my life? I couldn't help wondering.

It felt like he was here for a purpose. I hoped it wasn't some sort of cruel karmic payback.

I shook my head, squishing suds through my fingers. Get over yourself, I thought as I started to load plates into the dishwasher.

"What clan are you?" the clerk had asked. He might as well have asked me, "What planet are you from?" Obviously I wasn't from one of the Seven Clans, though it was interesting to think about. It would be kind of like finding out your real father was a famous celebrity who wanted you back. The Seven Great Clans were the celebrities of Wicca, supposedly possessing supernatural powers and thousands of years of shared history.

I rearranged the glasses in the top tier of the dishwasher. My book had said the Seven Clans stayed apart from the rest of humanity for so long that they actually had a separate and distinct genetic makeup. My parents . . . my family. We were as normal as they came. The clerk was just messing with me.

All of a sudden I dropped the sponge I'd been holding and stood up straight. I frowned and glanced out the window. It was dark. I glanced around the room, feeling a strong sense of . . . I wasn't sure what. A storm coming? Some vague feeling of danger was stirring the air.

I'd just snapped the dishwasher door shut when the kitchen door swung open. My parents stood there, my dad looking rattled and my mom tight-lipped and upset.

"What's wrong?" I said, turning off the water, feeling my heart begin to thump.

My mom ran her hand through her straight russet hair, so

like Mary K.'s. "Are these yours?" she asked. "These books about witches?" She held up the books I had bought at Practical Magick.

"Uh-huh," I said. "So what?"

"Why do you have them?" my mom asked. She hadn't changed out of her work clothes, and she looked rumpled and tired.

"It's interesting," I said, dumbfounded by her tone.

My parents looked at each other. The overhead light glinted off my dad's balding spot.

"Are kids at school into this, or is it just you?" my mom asked.

"Mary Grace," my dad said, but she ignored him.

I felt my brow furrow. "What do you mean? This isn't a big deal or anything, is it?" I shook my head. "It's just . . . interesting. I wanted to know more about it."

"Morgan," my mom began, and I couldn't believe how upset she looked. She almost always kept her cool with me and Mary K., no matter how crazed her life got.

"What your mother's trying to say," my dad offered, "is that these books about witchcraft are not the kind of thing we want you to be reading." He cleared his throat and tugged on the vee of his sweater vest, looking incredibly uncomfortable.

My mouth dropped open. "How come?" I asked.

"How come!" my mom snapped, and I almost jumped at the tone in her voice. "Because it's witchcraft!"

I stared at her. "But it's not like . . . black magic or anything," I tried to explain. "I mean, there's really nothing harmful or scary in it. It's just people hanging out, getting in touch with nature. So what if they celebrate full moons?" I didn't mention penis candles, bolts of energy, or naked swimming.

"It's more than that," my mom insisted. Her brown eyes were wide, and she looked as taut as a piano wire. She turned to my dad. "Sean, help me here."

"Look, Morgan," my dad said, more calmly. "We're concerned about this. I think we're pretty open-minded, but we're Catholics. That's our religion. We are part of the Catholic Church. The Catholic Church does not condone witchcraft or people who study witchcraft."

"I don't believe this," I said, starting to get impatient. "You're acting like this is a huge threat or something." Memories of how sick I had felt after the two circles flashed through my mind. "I mean, this is Wicca. It's like people deciding to protest animal testing or wanting to dance around a maypole." Some of the facts about Wicca that I had read in my book came back to me. "You know, the Catholic Church has adopted a bunch of traditions that began with Wicca. Like using mistletoe at Christmas and eggs at Easter. Those were both ancient symbols from a religion that began long before Christianity or Judaism."

My mom stared at me. "Look, miss," she said, and I knew she was really angry. "I'm telling you that we will not have witchcraft in this house. I'm telling you that the Catholic Church does not condone this. I'm telling you that we believe in *one* God. Now, I want these books out of this house!"

It was like my mom had been replaced by an alien duplicate. This sounded so unlike her that I just gaped. My dad stood next to her, his hand on her shoulder, obviously trying to get her to calm down, but she just glared at me, the lines around her mouth deep, her eyes angry and cold and ... worried?

I didn't know what to say. My mom was usually incredibly reasonable.

"I thought we believed in the Father, the Son, and the Holy Ghost," I said. "That's three."

Mom looked almost apoplectic, the veins in her neck jumping out. I suddenly realized that I was taller than she was now. "Go to your room!" she shouted, and again I jumped. We're not a raised-voice kind of family.

"Mary Grace," my dad murmured.

"Go!" my mom yelled, throwing out her arm and pointing out the kitchen door. It almost looked like she wanted to hit me, and I was way shocked.

Dad reached out his hand and touched Mom's shoulder in a tentative, ineffectual gesture. His face looked drawn and his eyes concerned behind their wire-rim glasses.

"I'm going," I muttered, taking the long way around her. I stomped upstairs to my room and slammed the door. I even locked it, which I'm not supposed to do. I sat on my bed, spooked and trying not to cry.

Over and over, I had the same thought: What is Mom so scared of?

14

Deeper

><"The king and queen longed for a child for many years and finally adopted an infant girl. But to their misfortune, the child was destined to grow enormous and devour them with her steely teeth."
—from a Russian fairy tale><

"So how come you're in the dollhouse?" Mary K. asked the next morning.

I backed Das Boot out of our driveway, two strawberry Pop-Tarts clenched between my teeth.

Once when Mary K. was little, she had done something bad, and my mom had sternly told her she was "in the doghouse." She had heard "dollhouse," and of course the whole thing made no sense to her. Now it's what we always say.

"I was reading some stuff they didn't want me to read," I muttered casually, trying not to spew crumbs all over my dashboard.

Mary K.'s eyes opened wide. "Like pornography?" she asked excitedly. "Where'd you get it?"

"It wasn't pornography," I told her in exasperation. "It was no big deal. I don't know why they're so upset."

"So what was it?" she persisted.

I rolled my eyes and shifted gears. "They were some books about Wicca," I said. "Which is an ancient, woman-based religion that predates Judaism and Christianity." I sounded like a textbook.

My sister thought about it for a few moments. "Well, *that's* boring," she said finally. "Why can't you read porn or something fun that I could borrow?"

I laughed. "Maybe later."

"You're kidding," Bree said, her eyes wide. "I don't believe it. That's awful."

"It's so stupid," I said. "They said they want the books out of the house." The bench where we sat outside school was chilly, and the October sunlight seemed to grow feebler by the day.

Robbie nodded sympathetically. His parents were much stricter Catholics than mine. I doubted he'd shared his interest in Wicca with them.

"You can keep them at my house," Bree said. "My dad could care less."

I zipped my parka up around my neck and burrowed into it. There were only a few minutes before class started, and our new, hybrid clique was gathered by the east door of school. I could see Tamara and Janice walking up to the building, their heads bent as they talked. I missed them. I hadn't seen them much lately.

Cal was perched on the bench across from ours, sitting

next to Beth. He was wearing ancient cowboy boots, worn down at the heels. He was quiet, not looking at us, but I felt sure he was listening to every word of our conversation.

"Screw them," Raven said. "They can't tell you what to read. This isn't a police state."

Bree snorted. "Yeah. Let me be there when you tell Sean and Mary Grace to go screw themselves."

I couldn't help smiling.

"They're your parents," Cal said, suddenly breaking his silence. "Of course you love them and want to respect their feelings. If I were you, I'd feel miserable, too."

In that moment I fell deeper in love with Cal. On some level I guess I expected him to dismiss my parents as stupid and hysterical, the way everybody else had. Since he was the most ardent follower of Wicca, I expected my parents' reaction to annoy him the most.

Bree looked at me, and I prayed my feelings weren't written on my face. In fairy tales there's always one person who is made for one other, and they find each other and live happily ever after. Cal was my person. I couldn't imagine anyone more perfect. Yet what kind of sick fairy tale would it be if he was the one made exactly right for me and I wasn't right for him?

"It's a hard decision to make," Cal continued. Our group was starting to listen to him like he was an apostle, teaching us. "I'm lucky because Wicca is my family's religion." He considered this for a moment, his hand on his cheek. "If I told my mom I wanted to become Catholic, she would totally freak out. I don't know if I could do it." He smiled at me.

Robbie and Beth laughed.

"Anyway," Cal said, serious again, "everyone has to choose his or her own path. You need to decide what to do.

I hope you still want to explore Wicca, Morgan. I think you have a gift for it. But I'll understand if you can't."

The school door swung open with a bang, and Chris Holly walked out, followed by Trey Heywood.

"Oh," Chris said loudly. " 'Scuse me. Didn't mean to interrupt you *witches*."

"Piss off," Raven said in a bored tone.

Chris ignored her. "Are you casting spells right here? Is that allowed on school grounds?"

"Chris, please," said Bree, rubbing her temple. "Don't do this."

He turned on her. "You can't tell me what to do," he said. "You're not my girlfriend. Right?"

"Right," Bree said, looking at him angrily. "And this is one of the reasons why."

"Yeah, well—," Chris began, but was interrupted by the bell ringing and the appearance of Coach Ambrose striding up.

"Get to class, kids," he said automatically, pulling open the doors. Chris shot Bree an ugly look, then followed the coach inside.

I picked up my backpack and headed for the door, followed by Robbie. Bree lingered behind, and I glanced back quickly to see her talking to Cal, her hand on his arm. Raven was watching them with narrowed eyes.

Dazed, I found my way to homeroom like a cow returning to the barn. My life seemed very complicated.

That afternoon I put my Wicca books in a paper bag and brought them to Bree's house. She had promised I could come over and read them whenever I wanted.

"I'll keep them safe for you," she said.

"Thanks." I pushed my hair over my shoulder and rested my head against her door. "Maybe I could come over tonight after dinner? I'm halfway through the history of witchcraft book, and it's pretty fascinating."

"Of course," she said sympathetically. "Poor baby." She patted my shoulder. "Look, just lie low for a while, let it all blow over. And you know you can come over and read or just hang out anytime. Okay?"

"Okay," I said, giving her a hug. "How's the thing with Cal going?" It hurt to ask, but I knew it was what she wanted to talk about.

Bree made a face. "Two days ago he was happy to talk for almost an hour on the phone, but yesterday I asked him to drive out to Wingott's Farm with me and he turned me down. I'm going to have to start stalking him if he doesn't give in pretty soon."

"He'll give in," I predicted. "They always do."

"True," Bree agreed, her eyes wistful.

"Well, I'll call you later," I said, suddenly eager for this conversation to end.

"Hang in there, okay?" she called after me as I escaped.

The next week I made a point of hanging out more with Tamara, Janice, and Ben. I went to math club and tried really hard to care about functions, but I longed to be learning about Wicca and especially to be near Cal.

When I told my mom I had gotten rid of the books, she was faintly embarrassed but mostly relieved. For a moment I felt guilty for omitting the fact that the books were only at Bree's house and I was still reading them in the evenings, but

I chased the guilt away. I respected my parents, but I didn't agree with them.

"Thanks," she said quietly, and looked like she wanted to say more, but didn't. Several times that week I caught her watching me, and the weird thing was, it reminded me of the creepy clerk at Practical Magick. She was watching me with an air of expectation, as if I were about to sprout horns or something.

All that week autumn moved in slowly, sweeping up the Hudson River into Widow's Vale. The days were noticeably shorter, the wind brisker. There was a sense of anticipation all around me, in the leaves, the wind, the sunlight. I felt like something big was coming, but I didn't know what.

On Saturday afternoon the phone rang while I was doing homework. Cal, I thought before I grabbed the upstairs extension.

"Hey," he said, and the sound of his voice made me slightly breathless.

"Hey," I replied.

"Are you coming to the circle tonight?" he asked straight out. "It's going to be at Matt's house."

I had wrestled with this question for days. Granted, I was disobeying the spirit of my parents' orders by reading my Wicca books, but actually going to another circle seemed like a much bigger deal. Learning about Wicca was one thing; practicing it was another. "I can't," I said finally, almost wanting to cry.

Cal was quiet for a minute. "I promise you everyone will keep their clothes on." I could hear the humor in his voice, and I smiled. He paused again. "I promise I won't carry you into the water," he added so softly, I wasn't sure I'd actually heard it. I didn't know what to say. I could feel the blood racing through my arteries.

"Unless you want me to," he added just as quietly.

Bree, your best friend, is in love with him, I reminded myself, needing to break the spell. She has a chance. You do not.

"It's just that . . . I c-can't," I heard myself stammering weakly. I heard my mom moving around downstairs, and I went into my room and shut the door.

"Okay," he said simply, and let the silence, an intimate kind of silence, spread between us. I lay on my bed, looking at the flame-colored tree leaves outside my window. I realized I would have given up the rest of my life to have Cal lying there with me right then. I closed my eyes, and tears started seeping out to run sideways down my cheeks.

"Maybe another time," he said gently.

"Maybe," I said, trying to keep my voice steady. Maybe not, though, I thought in anguish.

"Morgan—"

"Yeah?"

Silence.

"Nothing. I'll see you on Monday at school. We'll miss you tonight."

We'll miss you. Not I'll miss you.

"Thanks," I said. I hung up the phone, turned my face into my pillow, and cried.

15

Killburn Abbey

><"There is power in the plants of the earth and the
animals, in every living thing, in weather, in time,
in motion. If you are in tune with the universe,
you can tap into its power."
—To Be a Witch, Sarah Morningstar, 1982><

Samhain is coming. Last night the circle was thin and
pale without her. I need her. I think she's the one.

"You know, some kids actually get pregnant when
they're sixteen," I muttered to Mary K. on Sunday afternoon. I couldn't believe my life had come to this: sitting in
the back of a school bus packed with a bunch of jolly, de-
vout Catholics on our way to Killburn Abbey. "They have
drug problems and total their parents' cars. They flunk out
of school. All I did was bring home a couple of *books*."

I sighed and leaned my head against the bus window,

torturing myself by wondering what had happened at the circle the night before.

If you've never spent an hour on a school bus with a bunch of grown-ups from your church, you have no idea how long an hour can be. My parents were sitting a few rows up, and they looked happy as pigs in mud, talking and laughing with their friends. Melinda Johnson, age five, got carsick, and we had to keep stopping to let her hang out the door.

"Here we are!" trilled Miss Hotchkiss at last, standing up in front as the bus lurched to a wheezy halt in front of what looked like a prison. Miss Hotchkiss is Father Hotchkiss's sister and keeps house for him.

Mary K. looked suspiciously out the window. "Is this a jail?" she whispered. "Are we here to be scared straight or something?"

I groaned and followed the crowd as they tromped off the bus. Outside, the air was chill and damp, and thick gray clouds scudded across the sky. I smelled rain and realized no birds were chirping.

In front of us were tall cement walls, at least nine feet high. They were stained from years of weather and dirt and crisscrossed by clinging vines. Set into one wall was a pair of large black doors, with heavy riveted studs and massive hinges.

"Okay, everyone," called Father Hotchkiss cheerfully. He strode up to the gate and rang the bell. In moments the door was answered by a woman wearing a name tag that said Karen Breems.

"Hello! You must be the group from St. Michael's," she said enthusiastically. "Welcome to Killburn Abbey. This is one of New York State's oldest cloistered convents. No nuns live here anymore—Sister Clement died back in 1987. Now it's a museum and a retreat center."

We stepped through the gates into a plantless courtyard covered with fine gravel that crunched under our feet. I found myself smiling as I looked around but didn't know why. Killburn Abbey was lifeless, gray, and lonely. But as I walked in, a deep, pervasive sense of calm came over me. My worries melted away in the face of its thick stone walls, bare courtyard, and caged windows.

"This feels like a prison," said Mary K., wrinkling her nose. "Those poor nuns."

"No, not a prison," I said, looking at the small windows set high up on the walls. "A sanctuary."

We saw the tiny stone cells where the nuns had slept on hard wooden cots covered with straw. There was a large, primitive kitchen with a huge oak worktable and enormous, battered pots and pans. If I squinted, I could see a black-robed nun, stirring herbs into boiling water, making medicinal teas for sisters who were ailing. A witch, I thought.

"The abbey was almost completely self-sufficient," Ms. Breems said, waving us out of the kitchen through a narrow wooden door. We stepped outside into a walled garden, now overgrown, sad, and neglected.

"They grew all their own vegetables and fruit, canning what they would need to last through a New York winter," Ms. Breems went on. "When the abbey first opened, they even kept sheep and goats for milk, meat, and wool. This area is their kitchen garden, walled off to keep out rabbits and deer. As is typical in many European abbeys, the herb garden was laid out as a small, circular maze."

Like the wheel of a year, I thought, counting eight main

spokes, now decrepit and sometimes indistinct. One for Samhain, one for Yule, one for Imbolc, then Ostara, Beltane, Litha, Lammas, and Mabon.

Of course, I was sure the nuns had never intended to use the Wiccan wheel in their garden design. They would have been totally horrified by it. But that's how Wicca was: ancient and gently permeating many facets of people's lives without their being aware of it.

As we walked down the crumbling stone paths, worn smooth by hundreds of years of sandaled feet, Mrs. Petrie, the herb gardener, was practically in rapture. I walked behind her, listening as she murmured, "Dill, yes, and look at that robust chamomile. Oh, and that is tansy; goodness, I hate tansy; it takes over everything. . . ."

As I followed her, I swear a wave of magick passed over me. It lifted my spirit and made the sun shine on my face. Each bed, though no longer tended, was a revelation.

I didn't know the names of most of the plants, but I got impressions of them. A few times I bent and touched their dried brown heads, their broken seedpods, their withered leaves. As I did, shadowy images formed in my mind: boneset, feverfew, eyebright, meadowsweet, rosemary, dandelion again and again.

Here in front of me were the sparse autumn remains of plants with the power to heal, to work magick, to flavor food, to make incense and soap and dye. . . . My head swirled with their possibilities.

Kneeling, I brushed my fingers against a pale aloe, which everyone uses to help with burns and sunburn. My mom used to all the time and didn't worry about witchcraft. A shrubby bay laurel bush stood nearby, its trunk twisted with time and age. When I touched it, it felt clean, pure, strong. There were thyme bushes; a huge, dying catnip; caraway seeds, tiny and brown on brittle stems. It was a new world for me to explore, to lose myself in. Tenderly I touched a gnarled spearmint plant.

"Mint never dies," Mrs. Petrie said, seeing me. "It always comes back. It's actually very invasive—I grow mine in pots."

I smiled and nodded at her, no longer feeling the chill of the air. I explored every path, seeing empty spaces where plants had been or where their stems still stood, awaiting their rebirth in the spring. I carefully read the small metal plates, each with a plant's name handwritten in a feminine, even cursive.

My mom came and stood next to me. "This is so interesting, isn't it?" I felt she was trying to make amends.

"It's incredible," I said sincerely. "I love all these herbs. Do you think Dad would give me a little space in the yard so we could grow our own?"

My mom looked into my eyes, brown into brown. "You're that interested?" she said, glancing down at a tough, woody clump of rosemary.

"Yeah," I said. "It's so pretty here. Wouldn't it be cool if we could cook with our own parsley and rosemary?"

"Yes, it would," my mom said. "Maybe next spring. We'll talk to Dad about it." She turned away and went to stand next to Miss Hotchkiss, who was discussing the history of the abbey.

When it was time to get back on the bus, I had to tear myself away. I wanted to stay at the abbey and walk its halls and smell its scents and feel the drying leaves of plants crumble beneath my fingertips. The plants called me with the magick of their thin, reedy life forces, and there, outside the gates of the Killburn Abbey, it came to me.

In spite of my parents' objections, in spite of everything, it wasn't enough for me to learn about witches. I wanted to be one.

16

Blood Witch

><"There is no choice about being a witch. Either you are or you aren't. It's in the blood."
—Tim McClellan, aka Feargus the Bright><

Frustration makes me want to howl. She isn't coming to me. I know I can't push her. Goddess, please give me a sign.

On Monday after school Robbie and I ditched chess club and went to Practical Magick. It was getting to be a real habit with me. I bought a book about using herbs and other plants in magick and also a beautiful blank book with a marbleized cover and heavy, cream-colored pages within. It would be my Book of Shadows. I planned to write down my feelings about Wicca, notes on our circle, everything I was thinking about.

Robbie bought a black penis candle that he thought was hysterical.

"Very amusing," I said. "That's going to make you popular with the chicks."

Robbie cackled.

We headed to Bree's house and hung out in her room. I lay on her bed and read my herb book while Robbie fiddled with Bree's stereo, checking out her latest CDs. Bree sat on the floor, painting her toenails, reading my book about the Seven Great Clans.

"This is so cool. Listen to this," she said as the doorbell rang downstairs. Moments later we heard Jenna and Matt's voices as they came upstairs.

"Hi!" Jenna said brightly, her pale blond hair swinging over her shoulder. "Gosh, it's so chilly outside. Where's Indian summer?"

"Come on in," Bree said. She glanced around her bedroom. "Maybe we should go down to the family room."

"I'm for staying here," Robbie said.

"Yeah. It's more private," I agreed, sitting up.

"Listen, guys," Bree announced. "I was just reading this book about the Seven Great Clans of Wicca."

"Ooh," Jenna said, pretending to shiver.

"'After practicing their craft for centuries, each of the Seven Great Clans came to work within a single domain of magick. At one end of the spectrum is the Woodbane clan, who became known for their dark work and their capacity for evil.'"

A real shiver went down my spine, but Matt wiggled his eyebrows and Robbie let out a diabolical laugh.

"That doesn't sound like Wicca," Jenna said, pulling off her jacket. "Remember? Everything you do comes back to you threefold. All that stuff Cal read last weekend. Bree, that color is fantastic. What's it called?"

Bree examined the polish bottle. "Celestial Blue."

"Very cool," Jenna said.

"Thanks," Bree said. "Hold on—this is really interesting. 'At the opposite end of the magickal spectrum is the Rowanwand clan. Ever good, ever peaceful, the Rowanwands became known for being the repository of much magickal knowledge. They wrote the first Book of Shadows. They gathered spells. They explored the magickal properties of the world around them.'"

"Cool," said Robbie. "What happened to them?"

Bree scanned down the page. "Um, let's see...."

"They died," came Cal's rich voice, from Bree's open door.

We all jumped—none of us had heard the doorbell ring or his tread on the stairs.

After her moment of surprise, Bree gave him a brilliant smile. "Come on in," she said, clearing her nail polish stuff away.

"Hey, Cal," Jenna said with a smile.

"Hey," he said, hanging his jacket on the doorknob.

"What do you mean, they died?" Robbie asked.

Cal came and sat next to me on the bed. Bree turned around and saw us sitting there together, and her eyes flickered.

"Well, there were Seven Great Clans," Cal reiterated. "The Woodbanes, who were considered evil, and the Rowanwands, who were considered good, and five other clans in between, who were various shades of good and evil."

"Is this a true story?" Jenna asked, throwing her gum into the trash.

Cal nodded. "As far as we know. Anyway, the Woodbanes and the Rowanwands basically warred with each other for thousands of years, and the other five clans were sometimes allied with one, sometimes with another, during that time."

"Who were the other five clans?" Robbie asked.

"Wait, hold on. I just saw it," Bree said, trailing her finger down a page.

"The Woodbanes, the Rowanwands, the Vikroths, the Brightendales, the Burnhides, the Wyndenkells, and the Leapvaughns," I recited from memory. Everyone looked at me in surprise, except Cal, who smiled slightly.

"I just read that book," I said.

Bree nodded slowly. "Yeah, Morgan's right. It says here the Vikroths were warrior types. The Brightendales worked mostly with plants and were sort of doctors. The Burnhides specialized in gem, crystal, and metal magick, and the Wyndenkells were expert spell writers. The Leapvaughns were mischievous and humorous and sometimes pretty awful."

"The Vikroths were related to the Vikings," Cal said. "And the word *leprechaun* is related to *Leapvaughn.*"

"Cool," Matt said. Jenna came and sat on the floor in front of him so she could lean back against his legs. His fingers absently played with her hair.

"So how did they die?" Robbie asked.

"They battled each other for thousands of years," Cal repeated. A strand of his hair shadowed one cheek. "Slowly their numbers dwindled. The Woodbanes and their allies simply killed their enemies, either by open warfare or through black spells. The Rowanwands also hurt their enemies, not so much with black magic but by hoarding knowledge, letting the other clans' lines of knowledge die out, refusing to share their wealth. Like, if members of the Vikroths became ill and the Rowanwands could cure them with a spell, they didn't. And so their enemies died."

"Those bastards," Robbie said, and Bree giggled. A tiny spark of irritation made me frown.

Cal shot Robbie a sardonic look.

"Go on, Cal," Bree said. "Don't mind him."

Outside, it had been dark for a while, and a cold, steady rain began to patter against the windowpanes. I hated the thought of having to go home to Mary K.'s hamburgers and french fries.

"Well, about three hundred years ago," Cal continued, "until the time of the Salem witch trials in this country, there was a huge cataclysm among the tribes. No one knows exactly why it happened just at that time, but all over the world, and the clans had spread a bit, witches were suddenly decimated. Over the course of a hundred years historians estimate that ninety to ninety-five percent of all witches were killed—either by each other or by the human authorities that had gotten involved in the conflict."

"Are you saying that the Salem witch trials were organized by other witches to destroy their rivals?" Bree asked incredulously.

"I'm saying that it isn't clear," Cal said. "It's a possibility."

On the outside my flesh felt warm, my senses soothed by Cal's presence and his voice. On the inside I felt cold to the bone. I hated hearing about witches dying, being persecuted.

"After that," Cal went on, "for over two hundred years witches everywhere fell into a Dark Age. The clans lost their cohesiveness; witches from different clans either intermarried and had children who belonged nowhere, or they married humans and couldn't have children."

I remembered reading that people thought the Seven Clans had kept to themselves for so long that they were different from other humans and couldn't reproduce with ordinary people.

"You know so much about all this stuff," said Jenna.

"I've been learning it for a long time," Cal explained.

Bree reached over and touched Cal's knee. "What happened then? I haven't gotten to that part yet."

"The old ways and the old resentments were forgotten," Cal said. "And human knowledge of magick was almost lost forever. Then, about a hundred years ago, a small group of witches, representing all seven clans or what remained of them, managed to emerge from the Dark Age and start a Renaissance of Wiccan culture." He shifted in place, and Bree's hand dropped. Matt was making a small braid in Jenna's hair, and Robbie was stretched on the carpet, one hand propping up his head.

"The book said they realized that the major clannishness of the tribes had helped cause the cataclysm," I put in. "So they decided to make just one big clan and not have distinctions anymore."

"Unity in diversity," Cal acknowledged. "They suggested interclan marriages and better witch-human relations. That small group of enlightened witches called themselves the High Council, and it's still around today. Nearly all of the modern-day covens exist because of them and their teachings. Nowadays Wicca is growing fast, but the old clans are only memories. Most people don't take them seriously anymore."

I remembered the clerk at Practical Magick asking me what my clan was, and I remembered something else he had said. "What's a blood witch?" I asked. "As opposed to a witch witch?"

Cal looked into my eyes, and I felt a wave rise and swell within me. "People say someone's a blood witch if they can reliably trace their heritage back to one of the seven clans," he explained. "A regular witch is someone who practices Wicca and lives by its tenets. They take their magickal energy from the life forces found everywhere. A blood witch tends to be a much greater conduit for this energy and to have greater powers."

"I guess we're all going to be witch witches," Jenna said with a smile. She pulled up her knees and crossed her arms in front of them, looking catlike and feminine.

Robbie nodded at her. "And we have almost a whole year to go," he said, pushing his glasses up on his nose. His face looked raw and inflamed, as if it hurt.

"Except me," Cal said easily. "I'm a blood witch."

"You're a blood witch?" Bree asked, her eyes wide.

"Sure." Cal shrugged. "My mom is; my dad was; so I am. There are more of us around than you think. My mom knows a bunch."

"Whoa," Matt said, his hands still as he stared at Cal. "So what clan are you?"

Cal grinned. "Don't know. The family records got lost when my parents' families emigrated to America. My mom's family was from Ireland, and my dad's family was from

Scotland, so they could have been from a bunch of different clans. Maybe Woodbane," he said, and laughed.

"That is so awesome," Jenna said. "It makes it seem so much more real."

"I'm not as powerful as a lot of witches are," Cal said matter-of-factly.

In my mind I traced the edge of his profile—smooth brow, straight nose, carved lips—and the rest of the room faded from view. I thought dimly, It's six o'clock, and then I heard the muffled notes of the clock downstairs striking the hour.

"I have to get home," I heard myself say, as if from a great distance. I tucked my herb book under my sweater. Then I pulled my gaze away from Cal's face and walked out of the room, feeling like I was sinking knee-deep into a sponge with every step.

On the way downstairs I gripped the handrail tightly. Outside, the rain swept across my face. I blinked and hurried toward Das Boot. My car was freezing inside, with icy vinyl seats and a cold steering wheel. My wet, cold hands turned the key in the starter.

The words kept throbbing in my head. *Blood witch. Blood witch. Blood witch.*

17

Trapped

><"In 1217 witchfinders imprisoned a Vikraut witch. Yet on the following morn the cell was empty. Thus comes the saying 'Better to kill a witch three times than to lock her up once,' for a witch cannot be contained."

—WITCHES, MAGES, AND WARLOCKS, Altus Polydarmus, 1618.><

October. I've put away my old journal. This is my first entry into my Book of Shadows. I don't know if I'm doing it right. I've never seen another BOS. But I wanted to document my coming alive, this autumn, this year. I'm coming alive as a witch, and it's the happiest and the scariest thing I've ever done.

"And it was just so amazing," I said, peeling the top off my yogurt. "The whole garden was laid out in eight spokes, like the sabbat wheel. All these plants for healing and cooking. And they were all nuns! Catholic nuns!" I spooned up some yogurt and looked around my lunch table.

We were in the school cafeteria, and Robbie had made the mistake of casually asking how the church trip had gone on Sunday—his family goes to my church. Now I wouldn't shut up about it.

"You gotta watch those nuns," Robbie said, drinking his milk shake.

"Gosh, it is just everywhere." Jenna shook her head. She wiped her lips with a paper napkin and pushed her hair back over her shoulders. "Now that I know about it, it seems like traces of Wicca are everywhere I look. My mom was talking about going up to Red Kill to buy a pumpkin for Halloween, and I realized where that tradition really comes from."

"Hey," said Ethan sleepily, sinking into a chair next to Sharon. "'Sup?" His eyes were red, and his long ringlets were clotted above his collar.

Sharon looked at him in disgust, edging away from him as if he would get dirt on her pristine tartan skirt and white oxford shirt. "Are you ever *not* stoned?" she asked.

"I'm not stoned *now*," Ethan said. "I have a cold."

I glanced over at him and could sense his muzzy headedness and stuffed-up sinuses.

"Ethan doesn't smoke anymore," Cal said quietly. "Right, Ethan?"

Ethan looked irritated and opened a can of cranberry juice from the school machine. "That's right, man. I get high on life," he said.

Cal laughed.

"Next you'll be telling me I have to be a damn vegetarian or something," Ethan grumbled.

"Anything but that," Robbie said sarcastically.

Sharon wiggled away from Ethan, looking prissy. Gold

bracelets clinked on her wrist, and she speared a piece of teriyaki chicken with a chopstick.

"Watch out for her cooties," Beth whispered to Ethan. Today she wore a diamond in her nose and another diamond bindi on her forehead. She looked exotic, her green eyes glowing catlike against her dark skin.

Sharon made a face at her as Ethan started laughing and choked on his juice.

Bree and I shared a look, then Bree's eyes fastened on Cal. Steadfastly I went back to eating my yogurt. We sat there, overflowing our lunch table designed to seat eight: me and Bree; Raven and Beth, with their nose rings and dyed hair and mehendi tattoos; Jenna and Matt, the perfect couple; Ethan and Robbie, scruffy and rough; Sharon Goodfine, stuck-up princess; and Cal, tying us all together, giving us something in common. He looked around the table at us, seeming happy to be here, glad to be with us. We were the privileged nine. His new coven, if we wanted to be.

I wanted to be.

"Morgan! Wait!" Jenna called as I headed to my car. It was Friday afternoon, another week gone. I waited for her to catch up and shifted my backpack to the other shoulder.

"Are you coming to the circle tomorrow night?" Jenna asked when she was close enough. "It's going to be at my house. I thought we could make sushi."

I felt like an alcoholic being offered a cold, strong drink. The thought of going to another circle, feeling the magick coiling through my veins, having that magickal intimacy with Cal, practically made me want to whimper.

"I really want to," I said hesitantly.

"Why wouldn't you come?" she asked, her eyes confused.

"You seem so interested in Wicca. And Cal said you have a gift for it."

I sighed. "My parents are totally against it," I explained. "I'm dying to come, but I just can't face the scene at home if I do."

"Tell them I'm having a party," Jenna said. "Or that you're sleeping over at my place. We missed you last week. It's more fun when you're there."

I grinned wryly. "You mean no one fell over, clutching her chest?"

She laughed. "No," she said. "But Cal said you were just extra sensitive, right?"

Matt walked up and put his hand around Jenna's waist, and she smiled up at him. I wondered if they ever fought, ever questioned their love for each other.

"That's me," I said. "Sensitive Morgan."

"Well, try to come if you can," Jenna said.

"Okay," I said. "I'll try. Thanks."

I got in my car, thinking how nice Jenna was and how I had never known it because before this we had always been in different social groups.

"We're just going to hang out. You want to come?" Mary K. asked me on Saturday night. "Jaycee's rented some cheesy movie, and we're going to eat popcorn and make fun of it."

I smiled at her. "Sounds almost irresistible. But somehow I'm managing to resist it. Bree and I may see a movie. Will Bakker be at Jaycee's?"

Mary K. shook her head. "No. He and his dad went to a Giants game in New Jersey."

"Are things okay with him?" I asked.

"Uh-huh." Mary K. brushed her hair until it was shiny and smooth, then looped it up in a ponytail in back. She looked adorable and casual, perfect for hanging out at a girlfriend's house.

Soon after Mary K. rode off into the chilly night to bike the half mile to Jaycee's house, my mom and dad came into the living room, all dressed up.

"Where's the show at?" I asked, propping my socked feet up on the couch.

"Where's the show playing," my mom corrected my grammar.

"That too," I said, and gave her a smile. She made a mock-disapproving face.

"Over in Burdocksville," she answered, fastening a pearl necklace around her neck. "At the community center. We should be back by eleven or so, and we told Mary K. we'd pick her up on the way home. Leave a note if you and Bree decide to go out."

"Okay," I said.

"Come on, Mary Grace, we're going to be late," my dad said.

"Bye, sweetie," my mom called. Then they were gone, and I was alone in the house. I ran upstairs and changed into an Indian-print top and a pair of gray pants. I brushed my hair hard and decided to leave it down. I even opened the bathroom drawer, looked at Mary K.'s huge collection of eye shadows and blushes and concealers. I had no idea what to do with most of the stuff and didn't have time to learn, so I just put on a layer of lip gloss and headed for the door.

Jenna lived in Hudson Estates, a fairly new subdivision filled with mansions. I grabbed my keys and a jacket and shoved my feet into my clogs. I was thinking, Circle, circle, circle, and my mind was spinning with excitement. As I was opening the door to leave, the phone rang.

To answer or not to answer? I lunged for the phone on the fourth ring, thinking it might be Jenna with a change of plans, but I suddenly knew even before I had the receiver to my ear that it was Ms. Fiorello, my mom's colleague. "Hello?" I said impatiently.

"Morgan? This is Betty Fiorello."

"Hi," I said, thinking, I know, I know.

"Hi, hon," she said. "Listen, I just got your mom on her cell phone, and she said you might be home."

"Uh-huh?" My heart was racing, my blood pounding. All I wanted was to see Cal, to feel the magick again flowing through me.

"Listen. I need to stop by and pick up some signs. Your mom said they were in the garage. I have two new listings, and I'm doing three open houses tomorrow, if you can believe it, and I seem to have run out of signs."

Ms. Fiorello has the most annoying voice in the world. I wanted to scream.

"Okay . . . ," I said politely.

"So is it all right if I come by in, say, forty-five minutes?" Ms. Fiorello asked.

I glanced at the clock frantically. "C-could you come a little earlier?" I asked. "I was, um, thinking of going to a movie."

"Oh. I'm sorry. I'll try. But I just have to wait for Mr. Fiorello to get home with the car," she said.

Crap, I thought. "I could leave the signs outside," I suggested. "In front of the garage."

"Oh, dear," said Ms. Fiorello, continuing to ruin my life.

"You know, I think I have to look through them myself. I'm not sure which ones I'll need until I see them."

My mom had about a hundred real estate signs in the garage. I couldn't pile them *all* outside. Thoughts flew through my head, but I couldn't see a way out. Dammit. "Well, I guess I don't absolutely have to go to the movie," I hinted ungraciously, hoping she'd take the hint.

She didn't. "I'm so sorry, dear. Was this a date?" she asked.

"No," I said sourly. I needed to hang up before I started screaming at her. "See you in forty-five minutes," I said curtly, and hung up the phone. I felt like crying. For a bitter minute I wondered if maybe my mom had put Ms. Fiorello up to this to check on me. No, that seemed unlikely.

While I waited for Ms. Fiorello, I cleaned the kitchen and started the dishwasher: Cinderella, getting very late for the ball. I put a load of my clothes into the washer. Then I played music really loud and sang along for a while at the top of my lungs. I put my wet clothes into the dryer and set the timer for forty-five minutes.

Finally, over an *hour* later, Ms. Fiorello showed up. I let her into the garage, and she poked around in my mom's signs for what felt like a lifetime. I sat on the garage steps glumly, my head in my hand. She picked out about eight signs, then cheerfully thanked me.

"No problem," I lied politely, letting her out. "'Bye, Ms. Fiorello."

"Good-bye, dear," she said.

By the time she left, it was almost ten o'clock. There was no point in driving twenty minutes to Jenna's house when the circle would already be under way. I couldn't just break in three-quarters of the way through.

As I collapsed on our living room sofa, my misery was compounded by the fear that I was falling too far behind the rest of the Wicca group to join in again. What if Cal gave up on me? What if they wouldn't let me come to another circle?

I felt almost desperate. I seized on an idea that had been floating around my brain for a while. If I couldn't explore Wicca with the group, I could at least work a little on my own. Then at least I could prove to Cal and the rest of them that I really was dedicated. I was going to try to do a magick spell. I even had an idea for a spell to try. The next day I would drive up to Practical Magick and buy the ingredients.

18

Consequences

><"Forget not that witches live among us as neighbors, and practice their craft in secret, even as we conduct honest, God-fearing lives."

—WITCHES, MAGES, AND WARLOCKS, Altus Polydarmus, 1618><

On Sunday my family and I went to church, then to the Widow's Diner for brunch. As soon as I got home, I called Jenna. She was out, so I left a message on her machine, explaining what happened the night before and apologizing for not making it to the circle. Then I called Bree, but she wasn't home, either. I left a message for her, too, trying not to imagine her at Cal's house, in Cal's room. After that I sat at the dining table for hours, doing homework and losing myself in complicated, tidy mathematical equations, so satisfying in their clear solutions, they seemed almost magickal themselves.

*   *   *

I stopped by Practical Magick just before it closed, at five that afternoon. I bought all the ingredients I needed, but I waited until later that night, until my parents and sister were already in bed, before I began my spell.

I left the door to my room open a crack so I could hear if my mom or dad or Mary K. suddenly stirred. I took out my book on herbal magick. Cal had said I was sensitive—that I had a gift for magick. I needed to know if that was true.

Opening the book *Herbal Rituals for the Beginner,* I flipped to "Clarifying the Skin."

I checked my list. Was it a waning moon? Check. In my reading I had learned that spells for gathering, calling, increasing, prosperity, and so on were done while the moon was waxing, or getting fuller. Spells for banishing, decreasing, limiting, and so on were done while the moon was waning. It sort of made sense if you thought about it.

The spell I chose specified catnip to increase beauty, cucumber and angelica to promote healing, chamomile and rosemary for purification.

My room is carpeted, but I found I could still make a chalk circle. Before closing the circle, I moved my book and everything else I would need into it. Three candles made enough light to read by. Next I trickled a line of salt around my circle and said, "With this salt, I purify my circle."

The rest of the spell consisted of crunching things up with a mortar and pestle, pouring boiling water (from a thermos) over the herbs in a measuring cup, and writing a person's name on a piece of paper and burning it over a candle. At exactly midnight I read the book's spell words in a whisper:

"So beauty in is beauty out,
This potion make your blemish nowt.
This healing water makes you pure,
And thus your beauty will endure."

I read this quickly while the clock downstairs was striking midnight. At the very last *bong* of the clock, I said the final word. In the next instant all the hairs on my arms stood up, the three candles went out, and a huge bolt of lightning made my room glow white. The next second brought a *boom* of thunder so loud, it reverberated in my chest.

I almost peed in my pants. I stared wildly out the window to see if the house had caught on fire, then I got to my feet and flicked on my lamp. We still had electricity.

My heart was crashing around my rib cage. On the one hand, it seemed so far-fetched and melodramatic that this would happen exactly when I was doing a spell, it was almost funny. On the other hand, I felt like God had seen what I was doing and sent a bolt of angry lightning to warn me off. You know that's crazy, I told myself, taking long, deep breaths to quiet my heart.

Quickly I cleaned up all my spell stuff. I poured my tincture into a small, clean Tupperware container and tucked it into my backpack. Within minutes I was in bed with the lights out.

Outside, it was pouring and thundering in our biggest autumn storm so far. And my heart was still pounding.

"Here, try this," I said casually to Robbie on Monday morning. I pushed the container into his hands.

"What is this?" he asked. "Salad dressing? What am I supposed to do with this?"

"It's a facial wash I got from my mom," I explained. "It works really well."

He looked at me, and I met his eyes for a few seconds before I looked away, wondering if I looked as guilty as I felt, not telling him the truth. In a sense, experimenting on him.

"Yeah, okay," he said, putting the capped container into his backpack.

"How was the circle on Saturday?" I whispered to Bree in homeroom. "I'm really sorry I missed it. I tried to call you to see how it went."

"Oh, I got your message," she said regretfully. "My dad and I went to the city yesterday, and I didn't get back till late. Sorry. Got my hair cut, though."

It looked exactly the same, maybe an eighth of an inch shorter.

"It looks great. Anyway, how are things with Cal?"

Her classic brows wrinkled a bit. "Cal is . . . elusive," she said finally. "He's playing hard to get. I've tried to be alone with him, but it's impossible."

I nodded, hoping my expression of sympathy was winning out over my feelings of relief.

"Yeah. It's starting to really annoy me," she said glumly.

I thought about telling her that I had done a spell for Robbie and that I was waiting to see what would happen. But I couldn't form the words, and it, along with my feelings for Cal, became another secret I kept from my best friend.

*   *   *

On Wednesday morning Bree and some of the other members of the circle were sitting on the benches as usual. When I walked up to them, Raven gave me a snide look, but Cal seemed completely sincere when he invited me to sit down.

"I really am sorry about Saturday," I said, mostly to Cal, I guess. "I was all set to drive over to Jenna's when this woman my mom works with called and insisted on dropping by to pick up some stuff. It took forever, and I was so frustrated—"

"I've heard your excuse already, and it's fairly lame," Raven interrupted.

I waited for Bree to step in and defend me in our traditional best-friend solidarity, but she was silent.

"Don't worry about it, Morgan," Cal said easily, washing away the awkwardness left hanging in the air.

At that moment Robbie appeared, and we all just stared. His skin looked better than it had since seventh grade.

Bree's dark eyes flicked to him, grazing his face and processing what she saw. "Robbie," she said. "God, you look terrific."

Robbie shrugged casually and dropped his backpack on the ground. I looked at him closely. His face was still broken out, but if his skin before had been a two on a scale of one to ten, with one being the worst, now it was up to a seven.

I saw Cal glance at him thoughtfully. Then he looked at me, as though assessing my involvement. It was like he knew everything. But he couldn't, didn't, so I kept quiet.

Keep it to yourself, I commanded Robbie silently. Don't tell anyone what I gave you. Inside, I was elated and flushed with a sense of awe. Had my spell potion really worked? What else could it be? Robbie had been seeing a dermatologist for years, with no visible improvement. Now he shows up after two days of my tincture and looks great. Did this mean I was actually a witch? No, it couldn't be that, I reminded myself. My parents weren't blood witches. I was safe from that. But maybe I did have a small gift for magick.

Jenna and Matt drifted toward us.

"Hey, guys," Jenna said. The October wind whipped her pale hair around her face, and she shivered and clutched her books tighter to her chest. "Hey, Robbie." She looked at him as if trying to figure out what was different.

"Hey, does anyone have a copy of *The Sound and the Fury*?" Matt asked, pushing his hands into the pockets of his black leather jacket. "I can't find mine, and I've got to read it for English."

"You can borrow mine," Raven said.

"Okay. Thanks," Matt said.

No one mentioned Robbie's appearance again, but Robbie kept looking at me. When at last I met his gaze squarely, he looked away.

By Friday, when Robbie's skin looked smooth and new and completely blemish free, when practically every student in school recognized that he was no longer a pizza face, when girls in his classes suddenly realized that hey, he wasn't bad-looking at all, he decided to tell everyone how it happened.

On Friday afternoon I was in my backyard, raking leaves or, rather, raking occasionally but mostly seeing stunning maple leaf after stunning leaf, picking them up, examining them, admiring the passionate blotch and smear of colors across their finely veined skin. Some were still half green, and

I imagined that they felt surprised to find themselves on the ground so soon. Some were almost completely dry and brown, yet with a defiant border of red or bloody tips as if they had raked the bark on the way down. Others were ablaze with autumn's fire of yellow, orange, and crimson, and some were very small still, too young to die, yet born too late to live.

I pressed my palm against a crisp leaf as big as my hand. Its colors felt warm against my skin, and with my eyes closed, I could feel impressions of warm summer days, the joy of being blown in the wind, the tenacious hanging on, and then the frightening, exhilarating release of autumn. Floating, finished, to the ground. The smell of earth, the joining to the earth.

Suddenly I blinked, sensing Cal.

"What is it telling you?" His voice floated toward me from the back steps. I startled like a rabbit and rocked backward on my heels. Looking up, I saw Mary K. at the back door, directing Cal, Bree, and Robbie to the backyard to find me.

I looked at them in the darkening afternoon. I glanced around for my leaf, but it was gone. I stood up, brushing off my hands and my seat.

"What's up?" I asked, looking from face to face.

"We need to talk to you," Bree said. She looked remote, even hurt, her full mouth pressed into a line.

"I told them," Robbie said bluntly. "I told them you gave me a homemade potion in a container, and it's fixed my skin. And I . . . I want to know what was in it."

My eyes opened wide in dismay. I felt like I was being judged. There was nothing to do but tell them the truth. "Catnip," I said reluctantly. "Catnip and chamomile and angelica and, um, rosemary and cucumber. Boiling water. Some other stuff."

"Eye of newt and skin of toad?" Cal teased.

"Was it a spell?" Bree asked, her forehead wrinkling.

I nodded, glancing down at my feet, kicking my clogs through the leaves. "Yeah. Just a beginner's spell. From a book." I looked up at Robbie. "I made sure it wouldn't have any harmful effects," I said. "I would never have given it to you if I thought it might harm you. Actually, I was pretty sure it wouldn't do anything at all."

He looked back at me. I realized that he had the potential to be good-looking, behind the clunky glasses and the lame haircut. His features had been obscured by his awful acne. His skin, now almost perfectly smooth, was etched very slightly with fine, white lines in a few places, as though it was still healing. I stared at it, fascinated by what I had apparently done.

"Tell us about it," Cal invited.

The screen door opened again, and my mom poked out her head. "Hey, honey. Dinner in fifteen," she called.

"Okay," I called back, and she went in, no doubt curious as to who the unfamiliar boy was.

"Morgan," Bree said.

"I don't know how to explain it," I said slowly, looking down at the leaves. "I told you about the abbey upstate with an herb garden. The garden . . . I felt like it spoke to me." My face got red at the far-fetched words. "I felt . . . like I wanted to study herbs more, know more about them."

"Know what, exactly?" Bree asked.

"I've been reading and reading about medicinal, magickal properties of herbs. Cal said I was . . . an energy conductor. I just wanted to see what would happen."

"And I was your guinea pig," Robbie said flatly.

I looked up at him, this Robbie I barely recognized. "I've been feeling really bad about missing two circles in a row. I wanted to work a little on my own. I decided to try a simple spell," I said. "I mean, I wasn't going to try to change the world. I didn't want anything huge or scary. I needed something small, something positive, something whose results I could evaluate pretty quickly."

"Like a science project," Robbie said.

"I knew it wouldn't hurt you," I insisted. "It was just ordinary herbs and water."

"And a spell," Cal said.

I nodded.

"When did you do it?" Bree asked.

"Sunday night, at midnight," I said. "I guess I was feeling pretty depressed about being stuck home Saturday night during the circle."

"Did anything happen when you did the spell?" asked Cal, looking at me with interest. I could feel Bree's anger.

I shrugged. "There was a storm." I didn't want to talk about the candles going out or the crack of thunder that had been so amazingly loud.

"So now you control the weather?" Bree said, hurt in her voice.

I winced. "I wasn't saying that."

"Obviously it's just some sort of weird coincidence," Bree said. "There's no way you could fix Robbie's skin, for God's sake. Cal, tell her. None of us could do something like that. *You* couldn't do something like that."

"No, I could," Cal contradicted mildly. "A lot of people

could, with enough training. Even if they weren't blood witches."

"But Morgan hasn't had *any* training," Bree said, her voice strained. "Have you?" she asked me.

"No, of course not," I said quietly.

"What we have here is an unusually gifted amateur," Cal said thoughtfully. "I'm actually glad this came up because we should talk about this stuff." He put his hand on my shoulder. "You're not allowed to perform a spell for someone without his or her knowledge," he said. "It's not a good idea, and it isn't safe. It isn't fair."

He looked uncharacteristically solemn, and I nodded, embarrassed.

"I'm really sorry, Robbie," I said. "I don't even know how to undo it. It was stupid."

"Jesus, I don't want you to undo it," Robbie said, alarmed. "It's just, I wish you had told me first. It kind of spooked me."

"Morgan, I really think you need to study more before you start doing spells," Cal went on. "It would be better if you saw the big picture instead of just little parts of it. It's all connected, you know, everything is connected, and everything you do affects everything else, so you've got to know what you're doing."

I nodded again, feeling horrible. I had been so impressed that my spell had worked, I hadn't even thought through all the far-reaching consequences.

"I'm not a high priest," Cal said, "but I can teach you what I know, and then you can go on to learn from someone else. If you want to."

"Yes, I want to," I said quickly. I glanced at Bree's face and wanted to take back the speed and certainty of my words.

"Samhain, Halloween, is eight days away," Cal said, dropping his hand. "Try to start coming to circles if you can. Think about it at least."

"Pretty intense, Rowlands." Robbie shook his head. "You're like the Tiger Woods of Wicca."

I couldn't help grinning. Bree's face was stiff.

My mom tapped on the window to tell me dinner was ready, and I nodded and waved.

"I'm sorry, Robbie," I said again. "I won't ever do anything like that again."

"Just ask me first," Robbie said, without anger.

We walked across the yard, and I led my three friends through the house and out the front door. "See you," I called to them as Cal met my eyes again.

Halloween was eight days away.

19

A Dream

><"Witches can fly on their enchanted broomsticks, fabricated not only for sweeping."
—WITCHES AND DEMONS,
Jean-Luc Bellefleur, 1817><

The signs are there. She must be a blood witch. Her skin is splitting, and white light is leaking through. It's beautiful and frightening in its power. I vow on this Book of Shadows that I have found her. I was right. Blessed be.

That night Aunt Eileen showed up unexpectedly for dinner. Afterward she hung out with me in the kitchen and helped me clean up.

Out of nowhere, as I was scraping plates into the disposal, I found myself blurting out: "How did you know you were gay?"

She looked as surprised as I felt. "I'm sorry," I rushed to add. "Forget I asked. It's none of my business."

"No, it's okay," she said, thinking. "That's a fair question." She considered her answer for a few moments. "I guess when I was growing up, I always felt kind of *different* somehow. I didn't feel like a boy or anything. I knew I was a girl, and that was fine with me. But I just didn't get the whole point of boys existing." Her nose wrinkled, and I laughed.

"But I don't think I really figured out I was gay until about eighth grade," she went on, "when I got a crush on someone."

I looked up. "A girl?"

"Yes. Of course the girl didn't feel the same way about me—and I never told her about it or acted on it. I was so embarrassed. I felt like a freak. I felt there was something terribly wrong with me, that I needed counseling or help. Even medicine."

"How awful," I said.

"It wasn't until college that I came to terms with it and finally admitted to myself and everyone else that I was gay. I had been seeing a therapist, and he helped me see that there really wasn't anything wrong with me. It's just how I was made."

Aunt Eileen made a wry face. "It wasn't easy. My parents—your grammy and pop-pop—were so horrified and upset. They just couldn't deal with it. They were so disappointed in me. It's hard, you know, when the way you are, the way you were born, just totally bewilders and embarrasses your own parents."

I didn't say anything but felt a spark of recognition at what she was saying.

"Anyway, they gave me a really hard time. Not to be

mean or because they didn't love me but because they didn't know how else to react. They're a lot better now, but I'm still not at all what they want me to be. They don't ever want to talk about my being gay or people I'm involved with. Denial." She shrugged. "I can't help that. I've found that the more I accept it and accept myself, the less friction I have in the rest of my life and the less stressed and unhappy I am."

I looked at her in admiration. "You've come a long way, baby," I said, and she laughed. She put her arm around my shoulders and squeezed.

"Thank God for your mom and dad and you and Mary K.," she said with feeling. "I don't know what I would do without you guys."

For the rest of the night I sat on the carpet of my room, thinking. I knew I wasn't gay, but I understood how my aunt felt. I was beginning to feel different from my family and even my friends, strongly drawn to something they couldn't accept.

Part of me felt if I allowed myself to become a witch, I'd be more relaxed, more natural, more powerful, more confident than I'd ever felt in my life. Part of me knew that if I did, I'd cause pain to the people I loved most.

That night I had a terrifying dream.

It was nighttime. The sky was streaked with broad bands of moonlight, highlighting clouds in shades of eggplant, dove gray, and indigo. The air was cold and I felt the chilly breeze on my face and bare arms as I flew over Widow's Vale. It was beautiful up there, calm and peaceful, with the wind rushing in my ears, my long hair streaming out behind me, my dress whipping around my legs and molding to the outline of my body.

Gradually I became aware of a voice calling me, a frightened voice. I circled the town, wheeling lower like a hawk, circling and diving and floating on great strong currents of air that buoyed my body. In the woods at the north edge of town, the voice was louder. I went lower still until the tops of the trees practically grazed my skin. At a clearing in the middle of the woods I sank down, landing gracefully on one foot.

The voice belonged to Bree. I followed it into the woods until I came to a boggy area, a place where an underground spring seeped sullenly up through the earth, not flowing strongly enough to make a creek but not drying, either. It provided just enough moisture for breeding mosquitoes, for fungus, for soft green molds glowing emerald in the moonlight.

Bree was stuck in the bog, her ankle trapped by a gnarled root. Gradually she was sinking, being sucked under inch by inch. By the time the sun rose, she would drown.

I held out my hand. My arm looked smooth and strong, defined by muscles and covered with silvery, moonlit skin. I clasped her outstretched hand, slippery with foul-smelling mud, and I heard the suck of the bog around her ankle.

Bree gasped in pain as the root gripped her ankle. "I can't!" she cried. "It hurts!"

I made waving motions with my free hand, my brow furrowed with concentration. I felt the ache in my chest that signaled magickal workings. I began to breathe hard, and my sweat felt cold in the night air. Bree was crying and asking me to let her go.

I waved my hand at the bog, willing the roots to set Bree loose, to uncoil themselves, to stretch and open and relax and set her free. All the while I pulled steadily on her hand, easing her out as if I were a midwife and Bree was being born out of the bog.

Then she cried out, her face alight, and we rose gracefully, effortlessly in the air together. Her dress and legs were covered in dark slime, and through our hands' contact I felt the throbbing pain of her ankle. But she was free. I flew with her to the edge of the woods and set her down. Rising into the air, I left her there, weeping with relief, watching me as I rose higher in the sky, higher and higher, until I was just a speck and dawn began to break.

Then I was in a dark, rough room, like a barn. I was an infant. Baby Morgan. A woman was sitting on a bale of straw, holding me in her arms. It wasn't my mom, but she was rocking me and saying, "My baby," over and over. I watched her with my round baby eyes, and I loved her and felt how she loved me.

I woke up, shaking and exhausted. I felt like I was battling the flu, as if I could lie down and sleep for a hundred years.

"You feeling better?" Mary K. asked that afternoon. I had gotten up and dressed around noon and had puttered around the house, doing laundry, taking out the recycling.

I thought about Cal and Bree and everyone having a circle tonight, and I was aching to go. Cal probably expected me to go after what had happened yesterday. In fact, I really *had* to go.

"Yeah," I answered Mary K. I picked up the phone to call Bree. "I just didn't sleep well, woke up all headachy."

Mary K. mixed herself some chocolate milk and zapped it in the microwave. "Yeah? So everything's okay?"

"Sure. Why?"

She leaned against the countertop and sipped her hot chocolate. "I feel like there's something going on lately," she said.

I cradled the undialed phone on my shoulder. "Like what?"

"Well, like all of a sudden I feel like you're doing stuff that I don't know about," Mary K. said. "Not that I have to know all about your life," she added hastily. "You're older; you've always done other stuff. I just mean—" She stopped and rubbed her forehead with her hand. "You're not doing drugs, are you?" she blurted out.

I suddenly saw how things looked from her fourteen-year-old perspective. True, she was an *old* fourteen-year-old, but still. I was her big sister, she had picked up on my tension, and she was worried.

"Oh, Mary K., for God's sake," I said, hugging her. "No, I'm not doing drugs. And I'm not having sex or shoplifting or anything like that. Promise."

She pulled back. "What were those books about that Mom got so upset over?" she asked point-blank.

"I told you. Wicca. Crunchy tree-hugger stuff," I said.

"Then why was she so upset?" Mary K. pressed.

I took a deep breath, then turned to face her. "Wicca is the religion of witches," I explained.

Her beautiful brown eyes, so like Mom's, widened. "Really?"

"It's just, like, living in tune with nature. Picking up on stuff that already exists all around you. The power of nature. Life forces."

"Morgan, isn't witchcraft like Satan worshipping?" Mary K. asked, horrified.

"It really, really isn't," I said urgently, looking her in the eyes. "There's no Satan at all in Wicca. And it's completely forbidden to work black magic or to try to cause harm to anyone.

Everything you send out into the world comes back to you threefold, so everyone tries to do good, always."

Mary K. still looked worried, but she was paying close attention.

"Look, in Wicca you basically just try to be a good person and live in harmony with nature and with other people," I said.

"And dance naked," she said, her eyes narrowing.

I rolled my eyes. "Not everyone does that, and for your info, I would rather be torn apart by wild animals. Wicca is all about what you are comfortable with, how much you want to participate. There's no animal sacrifice, no Satan worshipping, no dancing naked if you don't want to. No taking drugs, no pushing pins into voodoo dolls."

"Then why is Mom so freaked?" she countered.

I thought for a moment. "I think it's partly that she just doesn't know a lot about it. Partly it's that we're Catholic already, and she doesn't want me to change my religion. Other than that, I don't know. Her reaction was a lot stronger than I could believe. It just really pushes her buttons."

"Poor Mom," Mary K. murmured.

I frowned. "Look, I've been trying to respect Mom's feelings, but the more I know about Wicca, the more I know that it's not a bad thing. It's nothing to be afraid of. Mom will just have to believe me."

"This sucks," Mary K. said. "What should I do if they ask me?"

"Whatever you need to say is all right," I said. "I won't ask you to lie."

"Crap," she said. She shook her head, then rinsed out her

mug and put it in the sink. "We're going to dinner at Aunt Margaret's, you know. She called this morning before you were up."

"Oh, no, I don't think I can," I said, thinking of tonight's circle. I couldn't miss another one.

"Hi, sweetie. How are you feeling?" my mom asked, coming into the kitchen with a basket of laundry balanced on her hip.

"Much better. Listen, Mom, I can't go to dinner at Aunt Margaret's tonight," I said. "I promised Bree I would go to her place." The lie slipped out of my mouth as easily as that.

"Oh," my mom said. "Can you call Bree and cancel it? I know Margaret loves seeing you."

"I want to see her, too," I said. "But I already told Bree I'd help her with her math." When in doubt, pull out school-work.

"Oh. Well." She looked like she was having trouble deciding whether to push it. "I guess that's all right. You're sixteen, after all. I suppose you can't go to every family thing."

Now I felt like crap.

"I just promised Bree," I said lamely. "She got a D on her last exam, and she freaked." I was very aware of Mary K. watching this exchange and wished she weren't there.

"Okay," Mom said again. "Some other time."

"Okay," I said. With Mary K.'s gaze following me out of the room, I headed upstairs and flopped onto my bed, cradling my pillow.

20

Broken

><"Men are natural warriors, but a woman in battle
is truly bloodthirsty."

—Old Scottish saying><

The night surrounded Bree and me in the comfy interior of her car. Matt's house, where the circle would be, was about ten miles out of town. As soon as Bree picked me up, I sensed that she had a lot on her mind. So did I. After my dream last night I was actually relieved to see her safe and sound and, apart from her quietness, normal.

I thought about the thousands of hours we had spent in cars with each other, first with our parents or Bree's older brother, Ty, driving us, then, for the past year, driving ourselves. We'd had some of our best talks in cars, when it was just the two of us. It felt different tonight.

"Why didn't you tell me about the spell you put on Robbie?" Bree asked.

"I put a spell on the potion, not on Robbie," I clarified. "And I didn't tell anyone. I thought the whole thing was pointless. I was sure it wasn't going to work, and I didn't want to be embarrassed."

"Do you really believe that it worked?" she asked. Her dark eyes were on the road ahead, and Breezy's high beams cut through the night.

"I . . . I guess so," I said. "I mean, mostly because I can't think of what else could have done it. On Monday he had awful skin; now he looks great. I don't know what else to think."

"Do you think you're a blood witch?" she asked. I was starting to feel interrogated.

I laughed to relieve the tension. "Oh, please. Yeah, that's it. I'm a blood witch. Have you seen Sean and Mary Grace lately? They just bought a new pentacle to hang over our living room mantelpiece."

Bree was silent. I felt rough waves of tension and anger coming from her but couldn't pinpoint their source.

"What?" I said. "Bree, what are you thinking?"

"I don't know what to think," she said, and I noticed her knuckles were white on the leather-wrapped steering wheel. To my surprise, she pulled her car over onto the wide shoulder of Wheeler Road. She turned off the engine and shifted in her seat to look at me.

"I'm having trouble believing how two-faced you are."

I stared at her.

"You say you don't like Cal. It's okay for me to go after Cal. But the two of you are always talking, staring at each other intensely, like there's nobody else around."

I opened my mouth to reply, but she went on.

"He never looks at me like that," she added quietly, and the hurt in her face was plain. "I just don't get you," she went on. "You won't come to circles, but then you do spells behind everyone's back! Do you think you're better than we are? Do you think you're so special?"

Shock made me tongue-tied. "I'm coming to the circle *tonight*," I said. "And you know exactly why I didn't come for a couple of weeks—you know how freaked my parents were. That spell was just experimenting, playing. I had no idea how it would turn out."

"You experimented by doing something to Robbie?" Bree asked.

"Yes, I did! And that was wrong!" I practically shouted. "But I made him look a million times better than he did before. Why is that such a crime? Why isn't that a favor?"

We sat there in silence, Bree's anger coming off her in rays.

"Look," I said after a minute. "Even though it turned out well for him, I know I shouldn't have done the spell on Robbie. Cal said it wasn't allowed, and I understand why. It was a stupid mistake," I went on. "I've been confused and freaked out, and I just ... I just wanted to ... to *know*."

"Know what?" she spat.

"If I'm ... special. If I have some special gift."

She looked out the window, silent.

"I mean, I see people's *auras*. Jesus, Bree, *I healed Robbie's skin!* Don't you think that's a big thing?"

She shook her head, clenching her teeth. "You are out of your mind," she muttered.

This was not the Bree I knew. "What is it, Bree?" I asked, trying not to burst into angry tears. "Why are you so mad at me?"

She shrugged abruptly. "I feel like you're not being honest with me," she said, looking out the window again. "It's like I don't even know you anymore."

I didn't know what to say. "Bree, I told you before. I think you and Cal would be a good couple. I'm not flirting with him. I never call him. I never sit next to him."

"You don't need to. He always does those things to you," she said. "But why?"

"Because he wants me to be a witch."

"And why is that?" Bree asked. "He could care less if Robbie or I became witches. Why is he playing guessing games with you, carrying you into pools, telling you that you have a gift for this? Why are you doing spells? You're not even an official coven student, much less a witch."

"I don't know," I answered in frustration. "It's like something seems to be . . . waking up inside me. Something I didn't know was there. And I want to understand what it is . . . what I am."

Bree was quiet for several minutes. In the dark small sounds came to me: the faint ticking of my watch, Bree's breathing, the clicks of Breezy's metal as the car cooled. There was a black shadow rolling toward me, toward the car, and instinctively I braced myself. Then it hit.

"I don't want you to come tonight," Bree said.

I felt my throat close.

Bree picked a piece of lint off her silky blue pants and examined her fingernails. "I thought I wanted us to do this together," she said. "But I was wrong. What I really want is for

Wicca to be something *I* do. I'm the one who's gone to every circle. I'm the one who found Practical Magick. I want Wicca to be for me and Cal. With you around, he gets distracted. Especially since you made it look like you can do spells. I don't know how you really did it. But it's all Cal can talk about."

"I don't believe this," I whispered. "Jesus, Bree! Are you choosing Cal over *me*? Over our friendship?" Hot tears welled up in my eyes. Angrily I dashed them away, refusing to cry in front of her.

Bree seemed less upset than I was. "You would do the same thing if you loved Cal," she informed me.

"Bullshit!" I yelled as she started the car again. "That's bullshit! I wouldn't."

Bree made a U-turn in the middle of Wheeler Road.

"You know, you're going to realize how stupid you're being," I said bitterly. "When it comes to guys, you have the attention span of a *gnat*. Cal is just another in a long line. When you get tired of him and dump him, you'll miss me. And I won't be there."

This idea seemed to make Bree pause. Then she nodded firmly. "You'll get over it," she said. "After Cal and I are really going out and everything calms down, it'll be a whole different picture."

I stared at her. "You are delusional," I said hotly. "Where are we going?"

"I'm taking you home."

"To hell with that," I said, popping open my door. Bree, startled, slammed on the brakes, and I lurched forward, almost whacking my head on the dashboard. Quickly I unsnapped my seat belt and jumped out onto the road.

"Thanks for the lift, Bree." I slammed the door as hard as I could. Bree roared off, spinning a fast doughnut twenty yards down, then whizzing past me again on her way to Matt's. I stood alone by the side of the road, shaking with anger and hurt.

In the eleven years of best friendship that Bree and I'd gone through, we'd had our ups and downs. In first grade she'd had three chocolate cookies in her lunch, and I'd had two Fig Newtons. She rejected my offer of my Fig Newtons for her chocolate cookies, so I had just reached out and snatched them, cramming them into my mouth. I don't know who had been more appalled, me or her. We hadn't spoken for a whole, agonizing week but finally made up when I presented her with six sheets of handmade stationery, each of which I had monogrammed with a *B* in colored pencils.

In sixth grade she had wanted to cheat on my math test, and I had said no. We didn't speak for two days. She cheated off of Robbie's test, and it was never mentioned again.

Last year, in tenth grade, we'd gotten into our worst fight ever, over whether photography counted as a valid art form or whether any idiot with a camera could capture a stunning image every once in a while. I won't tell who took what position, but I will say it culminated in a horrible, screaming fight in my backyard until my mom came out and shouted at us to stop.

That time we didn't speak for two and a half weeks, until we finally each signed a document saying that on this issue, we would agree to disagree. I still have my copy of our promise.

It was cold. I zipped my jacket up to my chin and pulled up the hood. I started walking toward Matt's house but then realized that it was too far away. The tears began to run down my face, and I couldn't stop them. Why was Bree doing this to me? In frustration, I turned around and started the long walk home.

The sharp-edged moon was so close, I could see its craters. I listened to the sounds of the night: insects, animals, birds. My eyes and ears became still more attuned, and I let them. I could make out insects on trees twenty feet away in the darkness. I saw birds' nests high on branches with the soft, rounded heads of sleeping birds visible at the edge. I became aware of the fast-paced fluttery thumping of the baby birds' hearts in syncopated rhythm with the much slower, heavier thud of my own.

I turned the volume of my senses down. I squeezed my eyes shut, but the tears kept coming.

I didn't see how Bree and I would ever recover from this, and I cried about that. I cried because I knew this meant she and Cal would really get together; she would make it happen. And I really cried, my stomach hurting, because I thought this meant I had to close all the doors inside me that had so recently opened.

21

The Thin Line

><"Anytime you feel love for anything, be it stone, tree, lover, or child, you are touched by the Goddess's magick."

—SABINA FALCONWING,
in a San Francisco coffee shop, 1980><

Early the next morning the phone rang. It was Robbie. "What's going on?" he asked. "Last night Bree said you weren't going to come to circles anymore."

Bree's assumption that I would give in to her so easily filled me with fury. I swallowed it and said, "That isn't true. That's what she wants. It isn't what I want. Samhain is next Saturday, and I'll be there."

Robbie paused for a few seconds. "What's going on between you two? You're best friends."

"You don't want to know," I said tersely.

"You're right," he said. "I probably don't want to know. Anyway, we're meeting in the cornfields to the north of town, on the other side of the road from where Mabon was. We're going to meet at eleven-thirty, and if we decide we want to be initiated as students into a new coven, that will happen at midnight."

"Wow, okay. Are you ... are you going to do it?"

"We're not really supposed to talk about it or decide yet," Robbie explained. "Cal said to just think about it in a completely personal way. Oh, and everyone has to bring stuff. I volunteered you for flowers and apples."

"Thanks, Robbie," I said sincerely. "Do we have to wear anything special?"

"Black or orange," he said. "See you tomorrow."

"Okay, thanks."

Church that day was much as usual. Father Hotchkiss noted that it was best to have a defensive line without gaps so that evil would have no place to gain access to your soul.

I leaned across my mom to Mary K. "Note to self," I whispered. "No gaps for evil."

She hid her grin behind her program.

That day I felt hyper—tuned in to the service, despite Father Hotchkiss. I wondered if following Wicca meant I really, truly couldn't ever come to church again. I decided it wouldn't. I knew that I would miss church if I stopped coming, and I also knew that my parents would kill me. Later on in my life, if I had to choose between one or the other, I could do it then. I thought about what Paula Steen had said, about it's what you brought to something that mattered.

Today I listened to the hymns and to the massive European organ played by Mrs. Lavender, as it had been since my mom was a child. I loved the candles and the incense and the formal procession of gold-robed priests and white-clothed altar boys and girls. I had been an altar girl for a couple of years, and so had Mary K. It was all so comforting, so familiar.

After church and brunch at the Widow's Diner, I went to the grocery store with that week's shopping list. On my way, I hopped up to Red Kill, to Practical Magick. I didn't plan to buy anything and didn't see anyone I knew, but I stood in the book section, reading up about Samhain for a while. I decided to bring a black candle next Saturday since black is the color that helps ward off negativity. Meanly I was tempted to buy Bree a roomful of black candles.

My anger at her was still white-hot. I couldn't believe her incredibly arrogant notion that she could kick me out of the circle. It only highlighted the harsh fact that in our relationship, she had always been the leader. I had always been the follower. I saw that now, and it made me angry with myself, too.

I dreaded going to school the next day.

"May I help you?" A pleasant-faced older woman, inches shorter than me, stood smiling at me as I looked at candles.

I decided to jump in headfirst. "Um, yes. I need a black candle for Samhain," I said.

"Certainly." She nodded and reached for the black candle section. "You're lucky we still have some left. People have been snapping these up all week." She held up two different black candles: one a thick pillar about a foot tall, the other a long, slim taper about fourteen inches tall.

"Both of these would be appropriate," she said. "The pillar lasts longer, but the taper is very elegant, too."

The pillar was much more expensive.

"Um, I guess I'll take the . . . pillar," I said. I had meant to say taper, but it hadn't come out that way. The woman nodded knowingly.

"I think the pillar wants to go home with you," she said, as if it was normal for a candle to choose its owner. "Will this be all for you?"

"Yes." I followed her to the checkout, thinking how uncreepy she was and how much more I liked her than the other clerk.

"If I brought flowers on Samhain, what kind should I bring?" I asked her a little self-consciously.

She smiled as she rang up my purchase. "Whichever ones want you to buy them," she said cheerfully. Then she looked closely into my eyes, as if searching for something.

"Are you—" she began. "You must be the girl David was telling me about," she said thoughtfully.

"Who's David?"

"The other clerk here," she explained. "He said a young witch comes in here who pretends not to be a witch. It's you, isn't it? You're a friend of Cal's."

I was stunned. "Um . . ."

She smiled broadly. "Yep, it's you, all right. How nice to meet you. My name's Alyce. If you ever need anything, you just let me know. You're going to walk a difficult road for a while."

"How do you know that?" I blurted out.

She looked surprised as she put my candle into a bag. "I just do," she said. "The way *you* know things. You understand what I'm talking about."

I didn't say anything. I took my bag and practically flew from the store, equally fascinated and unnerved.

On Monday morning I went defiantly to the benches where the Wicca group gathered and sat down, dropping my backpack at my feet. Beyond looking surprised to see me, Bree ignored me.

"We missed you Saturday night," Jenna said.

"Bree said you weren't coming anymore," Ethan put in.

There. It was right out in the open. I felt Cal's eyes on me.

"No, I am coming. I want to be a witch," I said clearly. "I think I'm supposed to be."

Jenna giggled nervously. Cal smiled, and I smiled back at him, aware of how Bree's jaw tightened.

"That's cool," Ethan said. "Here, push over," he said to Sharon, nudging her thigh with his knee.

With a put-upon sigh Sharon made room, and Ethan grinned. I watched them, suddenly recognizing a certain awareness between them. It blew my mind: Sharon and Ethan? Could they be interested in each other?

"Uh-oh, an outlander," Matt muttered jokingly, and Raven smirked.

Tamara walked up.

"Hi," I said, genuinely pleased to see her.

"Hi," Tamara said, looking around at the group. "Hey, Morgan, did you do all the functions homework last weekend? I really got stuck on number three."

I thought back. "Yeah, I did it. You want to go over it?"

"That'd be great," she said.

I grabbed my backpack. "No problem. See you all later," I

said to the group, and followed Tamara inside to the school library. For the next ten minutes we worked on the problem, me and Tamara, and it was so nice. I felt almost normal.

"I'm glad you're coming to Samhain," Cal said.

I looked back to see him following me out of calculus class. My locker was outside the lunchroom, and I had to switch books before Wednesday's chem lab.

I nodded and spun my locker combination. "I've been reading up on it. I'm looking forward to it."

"You think you want to be initiated as a student," he stated. "You need to think about whether you want to be part of this new coven." Tiny lines crinkled around his eyes as he smiled and leaned against the locker next to mine. "I know it's complicated for you at home."

I let myself look deeply into his eyes. There was a tide there, and it was pulling me strongly.

"Yes, I want to be a student," I said. "Even if you aren't a high priest. And yes, I want to be in your new coven. I've agonized over this. My parents are terrified of Wicca. They don't want me to do it, but I can't let them make this decision for me any longer. I'm feeling more certain every day."

"Give yourself a chance to think about it," he advised.

"I hardly think about anything else," I admitted.

He held my eyes and nodded. "See you in physics." He pushed off and left me there with a tingly, fluttery feeling in my stomach.

Bree wasn't my friend anymore, and that gave me the space to ask a simple question I'd been terrified to ask myself. Could Cal love me the way I loved him? Could we be together?

"Quick! Quick! Give me the tape!" Mary K. said, waving her hands. She was up on a ladder in our dining room. My mom was due home soon, and we were decorating for her birthday.

"Hang on," I said, twisting the two streamers together. "Here."

"Dad's picking up Thai food?" Mary K. asked, taping the streamers in place.

"Yep. And Aunt Eileen is picking up the ice-cream cake."

"Yum."

I stood back. The dining room looked pretty festive.

"What's all this?" my mom asked, standing in the doorway.

Mary K. and I both screamed.

"What are you doing home?" I cried. "We're not ready yet!"

Mary K. waved her hands. "Shoo! Go upstairs! Change! We need ten more minutes!"

My mom looked around and laughed. "You two," she said, then she went to go change.

Mom's birthday was fun, and nothing went wrong. She opened her presents, exclaiming over the Celtic-knot pin I gave her, the CD from Mary K., the earrings from my dad, and two books from Eileen. She wasn't recognizable as the person who had screamed at me just a few weeks ago. I smiled as she cut her cake, feeling a sense of doom about what was coming up on Saturday. But tonight we were all happy.

On Thursday, I was slumped in a chair in the school library during study hall, reading the Samhain chapter in one of my books. Tamara came up and tipped the book back to see its title.

"Are you still doing this stuff?" she asked softly, friendly interest in her face.

I nodded. "It's really cool," I said, the words lame and inadequate. "We've been holding circles every week, although I haven't been able to get to many."

"What's it all about?" she asked. "What is Cal trying to do?"

I hesitated. "He's trying to find people who are interested in creating a new coven," I said.

Tamara's brown eyes grew wide. "*Coven* sounds pretty scary."

"Kind of," I admitted. "But that's just because of . . . bad publicity," I guessed. "It's not scary at all. His coven will be more like a . . . study group."

Tamara nodded, not seeming to know what to say.

"Want to go to a movie tomorrow night?" I asked suddenly.

Her face broke into a wide smile. "That would be great. Can I ask Janice, too?"

"Yeah. Let's see what's playing at the Meadowlark," I suggested.

"Cool," said Tamara. "See you later. Happy reading."

I grinned, feeling lighthearted as she sat down across the room.

A moment later, with no warning, Bree dropped into the chair next to me. I tensed. "Relax," she said. "I just wanted to tell you that phase one of Bree and Cal is complete. I need a little more time, and then you can come to circles all you want."

I stared at her. "What are you talking about?"

"He's given in," she said happily. "He's mine. Give me a few more weeks to solidify it, and this will all be behind us."

"You've got to be kidding," I said, sitting up straighter. "This will *never* be behind us. Don't you get it? You chose a guy over our friendship. I don't even know why you're talking to me now." I looked into her beautiful face, once as familiar as my own.

"I'm talking to you to tell you to quit overreacting." She stuck out her booted foot and tapped my knee gently. "We both said things we didn't mean, but we'll get over it. We always do. All I need is a little more time with Cal."

I shook my head. I just wanted her to leave.

"You know what I'm talking about," she said softly, watching my face. "Cal and I finally went to bed. So we're going out. In a few weeks we'll be a solid couple. Then you can come back to circles."

A piercing pain in my chest startled me, and I swallowed and rubbed my shirt between my nearly nonexistent breasts. Twenty lightning-flash images of Cal and Bree intertwined on his bed, lit candles surrounding them, zipped through my brain, leaving it feeling raw and wounded. Oh God.

"How nice for you," I managed, pleased with the steadiness of my voice. "But I don't care if you're screwing everyone in the circle. You can't tell me what to do. I will be at Samhain." Anger fueled the words spooling out of my mouth. "You see, Bree, the difference between us is that I really am interested in becoming a witch. Not just pretending to be so I can seduce a good-looking guy."

"When did you become such a bitch?" she asked.

I shrugged. "Maybe I hung out with you too long."

She unfolded herself from the chair and moved off with such feminine grace that I felt like a rock sitting there.

It's true what they say. There's a thin line between love and hate.

22

What I Am

>< "Beware the witches' new year, their night of
unholy rites. It falls before All Saints' Eve. On
that day, the line between this world and the next
is thin, easily broken."
—WITCHES, MAGES, AND WARLOCKS,
Altus Polydarmus, 1618 ><

Tonight I'm going to a circle, and nothing can stop me. I'm going to declare myself to be a student of Cal's coven. I know my life will change tonight. I sense it in every sight and sound.

"Where's Bree?" my mom asked as Mary K. and I got dressed in our costumes. We were going to the school Halloween party since we had finally admitted to being too old to go trick or treating. It was barely seven o'clock, and already our front porch had been besieged by small pirates, devils, princesses, brides, monsters, and yes, witches.

"Yeah, good question," Mary K. said, drawing a fake

Frankenstein scar on her cheek. "I haven't seen her all week."

"She's busy," I said casually, brushing my hair. "She has a new boyfriend."

My mom chuckled. "Bree certainly is a social butterfly."

That's one way of putting it, I thought sarcastically.

Mary K. looked at my outfit critically. "Is that it?"

"I couldn't decide," I admitted. I was dressed up as me. Me, all in black, but me nonetheless.

"For heaven's sake, let's paint your face at least," my mom clucked.

They painted my face as a daisy. Since I was wearing black jeans and a black top, I looked like a daisy on a wilted stem. But no matter. Mary K. and I went to school and danced to a really bad local band called The Ruffians. Someone had spiked the punch, but of course the teachers found out about it right away and dumped it in the parking lot. No one from the circle was there, but I saw Tamara and Janice, and I danced with Mary K., with Bakker, and with a couple of guys from my various math and science classes. It was fun. Not thrilling, but fun.

We were home by eleven-fifteen. Mom, Dad, and Mary K. went to bed, and I arranged some pillows in the traditional columnar lump in my bed before I washed my face and sneaked out into the chilly darkness.

Bree and I had sneaked out before, to do stupid things like go to the twenty-four-hour QuikStop to get doughnuts or something. It had always seemed so lighthearted, like an acceptable rite of passage.

Tonight the moon shone down brightly like a spotlight, the cold October wind went bone deep, and I felt very alone and confused. As I crept toward the dark driveway, our jack-o'-lantern sputtered out on the front porch. Without its cheerful candlelit grin it seemed somehow sinister and garish. Pagan and ancient and more powerful than you'd think a carved pumpkin could be.

I breathed the night air for a moment, looking around for signs of people stirring. It came to me to try something—to sort of throw my senses out in a net, out into the world. As if they would pick up signals, like a TV antenna would or a satellite dish. I closed my eyes for a minute, listening. I heard—almost felt—dry, crumpled leaves floating to the ground. I heard the squirrels frantically scrambling. I felt the breeze carrying mist off the river. But my senses found no sign of parents or neighbors stirring. All was quiet on my street. For the moment I was safe.

My car weighs a ton, and it was hard to push it out of the driveway by myself, trying to steer and having to jump in and stomp on the brakes. I prayed some Halloween joyriders wouldn't come screeching around my corner and cream my car. I closed my eyes again for a moment, thinking about my house, and I sensed people sleeping calmly, breathing deeply, unaware I was gone.

Finally my car was in the street, facing forward, and easier to push and control. I moved it as far as the Herndons' house, with its new ramp for Mr. Herndon's wheelchair. I got in and started the engine, thinking about the heated seats in Breezy. In my hands Das Boot felt like a living animal, purring to life, excited to be eating up the road beneath its wheels. We drove off into the darkness.

I parked under the huge willow oak in the field across from the cornfields. Robbie's red Beetle was there, and so was Matt's pickup. I had already seen Bree's and Raven's cars on the other side of the road. Feeling nervous, I got out of Das Boot and walked around to the trunk. I looked over my shoulders constantly, as if expecting Bree—or worse—to leap out at me from the dark velvet shadows. Quickly I unpacked the flowers, fruit, and candle I had brought and set off to the cornfields across the road.

Even at this late, late date I still felt some uncertainty, despite what I had told Bree and the others about being a witch. Everything in my heart was a go for launching myself into Wicca, but my mind was still busily gathering information. And my heart was more fragile than it might have been, bruised from my fight with Bree, from thinking about her with Cal, from hiding all of this from my parents. I was truly torn, and at the edge of the cornfield I almost dropped everything, turned around, and ran back to Das Boot.

Then I heard the music, Celtic music, floating airily toward me on the breeze, a caressing ribbon of sound seeming to promise peace and calm and welcome. I plunged into the tall feed corn that had been left to dry on the stalk. It didn't occur to me to wonder where I was going or how I knew where to meet the others. I just went, and after brushing through the crackling golden sea, I found myself in a clearing, and the circle was waiting for me.

"Morgan!" Jenna said happily, holding out her hands to me. She was glowing, and her normally pretty face looked beautiful in the bright moonlight.

"Hi," I said self-consciously. The nine of us stood there, looking at one another. To me it felt like we had gathered to begin a journey together, as if we were going to climb Everest. As if some of us might not make it all the way, but we were together at the beginning. Suddenly these people seemed like total strangers. Robbie was distant and newly handsome, not the math geek I had known for so long. Bree was a cold, lovely statue of the best friend I had once had. The others I had never been close to. What was I doing?

My leg muscles tensed, ready for flight, and then Cal walked over, and I was rooted to the spot.

Helplessly I smiled at Jenna and Robbie and Matt.

"Where do I put this?" I asked, holding up my stuff.

"On the altar," Cal said, coming forward. His eyes met mine for a timeless, suspended second. "I'm glad you came."

I gazed stupidly into his face for the split second it took me to remember about him and Bree, what she had told me, then I nodded curtly. "Where's the altar?"

"This way. And happy Samhain, everyone," Cal said, motioning for us to follow him through the corn. When the moonlight caught his glossy hair, it glowed, and he did indeed look like the pagan god of the forest I had read about. Do you belong to Bree now? I asked him silently.

After we left the cornfield, there was a broad mowed meadow sloping gently downhill. In the spring it would be covered with flowers. Now it was brown and soft underfoot. At the bottom of the meadow there was a tiny, icy stream, clear as rainwater, flowing swiftly over smooth gray and green rocks. We stepped across easily, Cal going first and helping everyone else. His hand felt warm and sure around mine.

Since I had arrived, I had been watching Cal and Bree out of the corner of my eye. The knowledge that they had gone to bed together was inescapable. And yet tonight he at least seemed the same. Somewhat cool and remote, seeming to pay no special attention to Bree. They didn't look like a couple, like Jenna and Matt. Bree seemed high-strung, and even worse, she seemed more friendly toward Raven and Beth.

Past the stream the ground rose again and was swallowed into a line of thick trees. The trees were old, with gnarled bark, huge, spreading roots, and limbs as big around as barrels. Under the trees the darkness was almost impenetrable, yet I saw clearly and had no trouble picking my way through the underbrush.

Once we were through the trees, we found ourselves in an old cemetery.

I saw Robbie blinking. Raven and Beth shared amused smiles, and Jenna slipped her hand into Matt's. Ethan snorted but stepped closer to Sharon when she looked unsure. I knew Bree was feeling confused only because I can decipher almost every nuance of her expression.

"This is an old Methodist graveyard," Cal told us, resting his hand nonchalantly on a tall tombstone carved in the shape of a cross. "Graveyards are good places to celebrate Samhain. Tonight we honor those who have passed before us, and we acknowledge that one day we too shall pass into dust, only to be reborn."

Cal turned and led the way down a row of tombstones to what looked like a large, raised sarcophagus. A huge old stone, lichened and stained with hundreds of years of rain and snow and wind, covered a raised granite box. Its carved letters were impossible to make out even in the bright moonlight.

"This is our altar for tonight," Cal said, reaching down and opening a duffel bag. He handed a cloth to Sharon. "Could you spread this out, please?"

Sharon took it and spread it gingerly over the sarcophagus. Cal handed Ethan two large brass candlesticks, and Ethan set them on the altar.

"Jenna? Robbie? Can you arrange all the fruit and stuff?" Cal asked.

They gathered the offerings we had brought, and Jenna arranged it artistically on the altar in a cornucopia effect. There were apples, winter squashes, a pumpkin, and a bowl of nuts Bree had brought.

I took my flowers and Jenna's and Sharon's and put them into glass vases at either side of the altar. Beth gathered some boughs of dried autumn leaves and arranged them on the altar behind the food. Raven collected the other candles people had brought, including my black pillar, and fixed them to the sarcophagus by dripping wax and setting them on it. Matt lit all the candles in turn. There was hardly any wind here, and they barely flickered in the night. When the candles were lit, the place seemed more threatening somehow. I liked the idea of being able to hide in the darkness and felt exposed and vulnerable with the candlelight reflecting on my face.

"Now, everyone gather here in the middle," Cal instructed. "Jenna? Raven? Would you like to draw our circle and purify it?"

I was jealous he had chosen them—probably we all were. Cal watched the two girls patiently, ready to help if necessary. But they worked carefully together, and soon the circle was cast and purified with water, air, fire, and earth.

Now that I was again with a circle, I felt exultant, expectant. The only thing that marred my good mood was Bree's dark brooding and Raven's air of superiority. I tried to ignore them, to focus only on magick, my magick, and to open myself to perceptions from any source beyond my five senses.

"Our circle is now cast," Jenna said with awe in her voice. We all moved outward to stand just within its boundary. I made certain that I was between Matt and Robbie, two positive forces who wouldn't distract or upset me.

Cal took a small bottle and uncorked it. Moving deasil, clockwise, around the circle, he dipped his finger into it and drew a pentacle, a five-pointed star within a circle, on each of our foreheads.

"What is this?" I asked, the only person to speak.

Cal smiled faintly. "Salt water." He drew a pentacle on my forehead, his finger wet and gentle. Where he traced felt warm, as if it were glowing with power.

When he was finished, he took his place in the circle. "Tonight we're here to form a new coven," he said. "We gather to celebrate the Goddess and the God, to celebrate nature, to explore and create and worship magick, and to explore the magickal powers both within ourselves and without ourselves."

In the next moment of silence, I heard myself say, "Blessed be," and the others echoed it. Cal smiled.

"Anyone who wishes not to be of this coven, please break the circle now," Cal said.

No one moved.

"Welcome," Cal said. "Merry meet and blessed be. As we gather, so we'll be. The ten of us have found our haven, here within the Cirrus coven."

I thought, Cirrus? It was a nice name.

"You nine will now be inducted as novitiates, students of this coven," Cal explained. "I'll teach you what I know, then together we can seek out new teachers to take us further on our journey."

The only time I'd heard the word *novitiate* used was in relation to priests or nuns. I shifted on my feet, feeling the dense, soft ground beneath me. Overhead, the moon was high and white, huge. Every once in a while we heard the sound of a car or firecrackers. But in this place, in our circle, there was a deep, abiding silence, broken only by animals' night calls, the fluttering wings of bats and owls, the occasionally heard trickle of the stream.

Within myself I also felt a deep stillness. As if being put to bed one by one, my fears and uncertainties quieted. My senses were on full alert, and I felt incredibly alive. The candles, the breathing of the people with me, the scent of the flowers and fruit we had brought, all combined to create a wonderful, deep connection to Nature, the Goddess who is everywhere, all around us.

In the bowl of earth in the northern position, Cal lit an incense stick, and soon we were surrounded by the comforting scents of cinnamon and nutmeg. We joined hands. Unlike the other two times I had participated in a circle, tonight I was neither examining nor dreading what might happen. I kept my mind open.

Matt's and Robbie's hands were larger than mine; Matt's smooth and slender, Robbie's bulkier than Cal's had been. My eyes flicked to Robbie's face. It was smooth and unlined. I had done that, and within me I felt a recognition of and a pride in my own power.

Cal began the chant as we moved deasil around our circle.

"Tonight we bid the God farewell,
In the Underground he'll dwell.
Till his rebirth in springtime's sun,
But for now his life is done.

"We dance beneath the Blood Moon's shine,
This chant we'll sing to number nine.
We dance to let our heart's love flow,
To aid the Goddess in her sorrow."

I counted as we danced around the circle, and we chanted nine times. The more I studied Wicca, the more I realized that witches wove symbolism into just about everything: plants, numbers, days of the week, colors, times of the year, even fabrics, food, and flowers. Everything has a meaning. My job as a student would be to learn these symbols, to learn as much as I could about the nature surrounding me, and to weave myself into its pattern and magick.

As we chanted I thought about the end, when we would throw up our arms to release our energy. Once again I felt worried as I remembered the pain and nausea I had felt before. My facade of certainty began to crack, allowing in tendrils of fear. My power seemed scary.

Just as suddenly, as we whirled in our circle, singing the chant like a round, weaving our voices in and among one another, I realized that my *fear* would cause me pain if I didn't let it go right now. I breathed deeply, feeling the chant leave my throat, surrounded by the coven in our circle, and I tried to banish fear, banish limitations.

Faces were blurred. I felt out of control. I banish fear! The words of our chant slurred until it was a beautiful rhythm of pure sound, rising and falling and swirling around me. I was having trouble breathing, and my face was hot and damp with sweat. I wanted to throw off my jacket, throw off my shoes. I had to stop. I had to banish fear.

With one last burst of sound our circle stopped, and we threw our arms skyward. I felt a rush of energy whirling around me. My hand grasped the air, and I pushed my fist against my chest, seizing some energy for myself. I banish fear, I thought dreamily, and then the night exploded all around me.

I was dancing in the atmosphere, surrounded by stars, seeing motes of energy whizzing past me like microscopic comets. I could see the entire universe; all at once, every particle, every smile, every fly, every grain of sand was revealed to me and was infinitely beautiful.

When I breathed in, I breathed in the very essence of life, and I breathed out white light. It was beautiful, more than beautiful, but I didn't have the words to express it even to myself. I understood everything; I understood my place in the universe; I understood the path I had to follow.

Then I smiled and blinked and breathed out again, and I was standing in a darkened graveyard with nine high school friends, and tears were running down my face.

"Are you okay?" Robbie asked in concern, coming over to me.

At first it seemed he was speaking gibberish, but then I understood what he had said, and I nodded.

"It was so beautiful," I said lamely, my voice breaking. I felt unbearably diminished after my vision. I reached my finger out to touch Robbie's cheek. My finger left a warm pink line where it touched, and Robbie rubbed his cheek, looking confused.

The vases of flowers were on the altar, and I walked toward them, mesmerized by their beauty and also the overwhelming sadness of the flowers' deaths. I touched one bud, and it opened beneath my hand, blooming in death as it hadn't been allowed to in life. I heard Raven gasp and knew that Bree and Beth and Matt backed away from me then.

Then Cal was next to me. "Quit touching things," he said quietly, smiling. "Lie down and ground yourself."

He guided me to an open spot within our circle, and I lay down on my back, feeling the pulsing life of the earth centering me, easing the energy from me, making me feel more normal. My perceptions focused, and I saw the coven clearly, saw the candles, the stars, the fruit as themselves again and not as pulsing blobs of energy.

"What's happening to me?" I whispered. Cal sat down cross-legged behind me and lifted my head onto his lap, stroking my hair, which was strewn across his legs. Robbie knelt next to him. Ethan, Beth, and Sharon circled closer, peering over his shoulder at me as if I were a museum display. Jenna was holding Matt around his waist, as if she were afraid. Raven and Bree were the farthest back, and Bree looked wide-eyed and solemn.

"You made magick," Cal said, gazing at me with those endless dark gold eyes. "You're a blood witch."

My eyes opened wider as his face slowly blotted out the moon above me. With his eyes looking deeply into mine, he touched my mouth with his, and with a sense of shock I realized he was kissing me. My arms felt heavy as I moved them up to encircle his neck, and then I was kissing him back, and we were joined, and the magick crackled all around us.

In that moment of sheer happiness I didn't question what being a blood witch meant to me or my family or what Cal and I being together meant to Bree or Raven or anyone else. It would be my first lesson in magick, and it would be hard learned: seeing the big picture, not just a part of it.

sweep
Book Two

THE COVEN

*I am not who I thought I was. I am not a regular
sixteen-year-old girl. I am a witch. A real, ancestral witch.
My parents are not my biological parents.
My sister and I share no blood.*

• • •

*Even in the coven, I am too powerful now,
too different to belong.*

• • •

*I am alone except for Cal. Cal tells me he loves me,
and I need to believe him.*

• • •

ISBN 978-0-14-240987-9
Price $6.99 / CAN $8.99

sweep
Book Three

BLOOD WITCH

Every day, I learn more about magick.
The more I learn, the more my power grows.
Sometimes my own strength frightens me.

• • •

I know I'm not alone, though. Cal is with me,
my soul mate, my partner, my love.

• • •

Now I feel a shadow over us.
When I cast out my senses, I pick up danger.
But is it real, or is it all my mind?

• • •

ISBN 978-0-14-240988-6
Price $6.99 / CAN $8.99

sweep
𝔅ook 𝔣our

DARK MAGICK

I love Cal Blaire. He taught me about Wicca.
He helped me find out who I am.

• • •

But now we share a secret. A terrible, dark secret
that binds us together, even as it tears us apart.

• • •

I don't know Cal anymore. I don't even know myself.
And I don't know who or what to trust—except my magick.

• • •

ISBN 978-0-14-240989-3
Price $6.99 / CAN $8.99

sweep
Book Five

AWAKENING

Wicca has changed my life. I've lost old friends, made new ones. Discovered my true heritage. Found love—and betrayal.

• • •

But there's so much more to learn. I know Wicca can be used for good or for evil.

• • •

The hard part is knowing which is which.

• • •

ISBN 978-0-14-241020-2
Price $6.99 / CAN $8.99

sweep
Book Six

SPELLBOUND

It's almost Yule—the most joyous time of the year.
My magick is growing stronger. My friendships are flourishing.
I should be happy.

. . .

But a choice lies before me,
a decision that could change my world forever.

. . .

Am I strong enough to choose the right path?

. . .

ISBN 978-0-14-241021-9
Price $6.99 / CAN $8.99